THE HOPELESS ROMANTIC

Lola Walker

To all those who still believe in the power of love and the magic of
romance.

Content Considerations

T his book contains themes that may be upsetting to some readers. These themes include alcohol consumption, violence, death, domestic abuse, PTSD, sexual content, sexual assault, panic attacks, heartbreaks, anxiety and depression, graphic language, slight implication of trafficking, inaccurate and fabricated depictions of societies/kingdoms/people/cultures, body-shaming, homophobia, and narcissistic behaviors.

Your mental health matters. Read with caution.

Also, please know that this novel is comical. The humor in this novel is multifaceted, offering a variety of comedic elements. From quirky characters to absurd situations, the novel provides a range of comedic styles that cater to different tastes.

Contents

Chapter 1

*B*RRRING! Diana's alarm clock rudely let her know it was three in the afternoon and time to get her day started. It might seem late to some, but for her, it was the beginning of her productive hours. She had gotten lucky with a "fabulous," low-paying job at a crummy call center for a shark insurance company. Yep, that's right. An Australian shark insurance company that only existed in Detroit, Michigan.

She had graduated cum laude with a Bachelor of Arts in creative writing and an Associate's in liberal arts. Of course, when you don't have enough experience or connections, guess what? You're fucked. Time had only proven to her that you no longer needed a degree to make it in life. It was all about who you knew—and being an extreme introvert didn't help.

She considered herself lucky when she first got hired. No one understood how she landed that job or even knew that shark insurance existed. Oh, but it does. You wouldn't believe how many imbeciles and maniacs love to dive into shark-infested waters. When they inevitably get attacked by a big fish, there is some poor schmuck who must deal with their stupidity and make sure they're sufficiently compensated—as long as they have insurance, that is.

The type of job didn't matter to Diana. She was desperate. After many months of unsuccessful job hunting, she gave up on finding work with a publishing company. All she cared about was finding something that paid her share of the expenses with her boyfriend, Tom. She had hoped to follow her dreams, but the odds never looked good. As much as she loathed her position as a claims adjuster for shark "victims," she grew comfortable in its web of misery. If the pay was enough to sustain her lifestyle in the big city, then why keep setting herself up for rejection? She had always lacked confidence, possibly the result of growing up in a small town where being different was discouraged.

She feared new opportunities. Taking on risks wasn't worth the trouble because, to her, the setbacks were more than temporary. Most people say, "If at first you don't succeed, try, try again." In Diana's case, it was, "If at first you don't succeed, you will get ridiculed, smacked, and shamed. You will never try again because it would be an embarrassment."

From a young age, she had been a "failure" until proven otherwise, according to her parents. She always brought home good grades, but that was insignificant. It was simply an expectation... or else. Nothing she did ever impressed them. In their home, a "good girl" keeps her mouth shut, cleans the house, cooks the food, and eats last. She was grateful that she pushed herself to finish college, but it hardly felt like an accomplishment because she was not using her degree.

Diana rolled off her half-made bed, her eyes scanning the room, taking in the cold and lonely atmosphere. Despite the emptiness, she recalled that Tom was likely on campus. *It's still pretty early... the least I can do is pick up the place, fold his laundry, and make sure dinner is ready for him by the time he comes back.*

She couldn't help but imagine the amount of stress he was under as he prepared to take the Bar Exam a second time. The memory of his reaction to receiving his results last July haunted her mind. He stormed into their bedroom and locked her out for the entire day. She was not aware that he had blamed her for his failure until they had an argument that next morning.

Because Diana's unusual work hours made most social events impossible, she often craved his attention. They had most weekends off together, but wanting some quality time was too much to ask. Apparently, she was the reason he could never study. She promised him that she would give him all the space that he needed to study and pass. Things seemed to have improved after their last heart-to-heart conversation, whenever that was. Lately, though, she had been sensing more distance between them.

They still loved each other. After all, they'd been together for eight years, right? She hoped and prayed that he would pass his test with flying colors and then afterward, they could finally move forward in their relationship. *He'll pass, he'll be stress-free, he'll get his dream job, and then who knows . . . perhaps a proposal?* The thought excited her until she realized she was getting ahead of herself.

With the chores completed, she grabbed her phone to check the time. *Five-fifteen. He should be on his way now.* She took one final glance at the table that she had beautifully set for him and cracked a smile. She wanted to surprise him with his favorite meal, spaghetti al limone with shrimp. Like her, he was half-Italian and enjoyed authentic Italian cuisine. Next to his foiled plate, she had left a note: *You are the greatest boyfriend a girl could ask for. P.S. There is a surprise for you in the fridge.*

A special meal like this was never complete without dessert, especially if that dessert was strawberry shortcake (his favorite). It wasn't his birthday or anything; Diana just wanted to make him feel special. She wanted him to know how much she valued and appreciated him. Plus, a little gift-giving could reassure him that she still loved him deeply.

The night before yesterday was a complete disaster. She didn't mean to start another fight. *Is it such a crime to ask your boyfriend where he's going on his day off?* She went from being "nosey" to "accusatory," according to Tom. For what? She had no idea. She shook her head, as if that could erase the memory of their most recent argument.

"Just what are you insinuating?"

"You're gone all the time. I miss you, is all—"

"Then stop asking me these stupid questions! Studying! I'm always studying! You always do this!"

"Do what?"

"Diana, you better not fuck this up for me again. I have worked too damn hard to get this far!"

"I'm really sorry. I didn't mean to—"

"I'll see you later. Don't ask me where I'm going again."

She had not seen him since, but she knew his usual schedule. Diana didn't think much of his absence, as she was also pulling twelve-hour shifts. She glanced around the apartment for reassurance. Their entire place was immaculate and smelled of lavender Fabuloso. *Things will get better. If you are kind to others, sooner or later, they will reciprocate. Right? Nope, not if you live with a shithead narcissist.* She tried not to think of him that way, so she did everything she could to keep that "spark" in their relationship. In her mind, he was simply going through a phase. *Stress can do that. It can make you cruel.*

She circled back into her bedroom to see whether she had missed anything. *Whew, I almost forgot! If Tom found out about this one, he'd have another conniption!* She kicked her book under her nightstand. Romance novels was another issue. At first, her "addiction" added a little excitement to their relationship. But as soon as Tom found out, he accused Diana of "worshipping" fictional men and comparing him to them. He made her promise to limit her reading time.

Who would have thought that books would make a man so jealous? Reading was an escape for her. It was a way for her to feel the romance and love that she lacked in real life. Of course, she denied she was unhappy by convincing herself that true love only existed in fairytales. *A girl can dream.* She never gave up her passion for finding the greatest romance novels. She just hid them well.

***

It was a short drive to work. Before she climbed out of her car, she took a deep breath and shut her eyes. She held her hands together in prayer. Her Nissan Versa was her safe space, her confessional.

"Dear Jesus, please let me survive another shift. I'm grateful that I'm still making money, but you know that I do not want to work here forever. Please forgive my eye-rolling, my occasional yet discreet laughing, and my ill feelings toward my boss. People are assholes. I should know better than to stoop to their level. Please let today be a good day. Amen!"

She took another deep breath, walked into the building, scanned her ID card to punch in, and rushed to her cubicle to log on. Her job had a ridiculous new policy. All employees had to clock in at the precise shift time with only three minutes to log onto their computers. Computer lag time was never a viable excuse, even though it was a common issue for her. Her boss, Brenda, ignored Diana's complaints and tickets to technical support. Brenda always questioned why it was only Diana who was having computer issues. Even though Diana never called in sick and always accepted overtime requests, Brenda either thought she was lazy or simply had some inexplicable, unreasonable hatred reserved just for her.

Diana glanced at her schedule and rolled her eyes. *Figures. I have to take all incoming calls today. Great.* Instead of being assigned some of the other tasks available throughout the week, she had been scheduled to do nothing but take calls the past few months. Even though it was a good ol' December winter in Michigan, it was a balmy summer in Australia. Having their company headquarters in Michigan seemed unusual, but the company's CEO was a "global citizen." At least, that was the only explanation ever offered when someone thought to question such a bold business decision.

"At least today tomorrow is Friday," she muttered to herself as she clicked hard on her mouse. "Just two more days of bullshit."

She felt her anxiety rising as she opened the call software. Twenty clients were already waiting in the queue. She clicked on the Ready button to accept her first incoming call. When the line beeped, she recited the mandatory greeting. "Thank you for calling Sail-Co. As a reminder, this call may be monitored or recorded. My name is Diana—"

"You little bitch!" shouted a combative man from the other end of the line. "I have been calling your company to get a status on my check for the past three days!"

Her heart began to race. It didn't matter that she had two years of experience handling these calls. Dealing with confrontation was not one of her best qualities. No amount of yoga classes or holistic remedies could reduce her constant fear of a customer jumping out of the phone and blowing her head off.

"Excuse me, sir," Her voice shook. "If you're going to continue to use further profanity, I will disconnect the call."

"Fine," he grunted. "Go on! Say what you gotta say!"

She took a deep breath before continuing calmly. "So I can better assist you, you'll need to provide me your claim number."

He screamed out the numbers as she punched them into the system. "K! Five! Seven! Two! Four! Four! Nine! P!"

As usual, the system took forever to load. Diana started to sweat as she repeatedly clicked the button on the top of her pen with her thumb. *Fuck me! Fuck my life into pieces. . . . Oh, finally!*

"Okay, is this Mr. Anderson?"

"Yes!" he barked.

She rolled her eyes; this call was not going to end well. A notification in red bold letters alerted her of his medical coverage being denied.

"I have the claim in front of me now," she gulped. "I'm reading what was previously handled. Bear with me."

"Oh, come on!" he yelled.

"Sorry. Give me a moment, sir."

Diana scrolled down to review the file notes and it appeared that her co-worker, Gwenyth, handled the claim last week. She was stationed only a few cubicles across from her. One glance over showed she was not at her desk. *Come on, Gwen! You should have known better than to promise the customer any money, especially if a higher-ranked specialist had previously informed him of the coverage denial!*

"Mr. Anderson, it appears that the medical expense coverage had been previously denied and we informed you of this on December First."

"Oh yeah," he retaliated with a snooty tone, "then why did Gwen tell me otherwise?"

"Sir, Gwen is not a licensed specialist. She has no authority to—"

"Why are you people giving me the run-around?" he screamed. "I was attacked! What's the point of having you as my insurance company! You're all a bunch of con artists!"

Diana had to be blunt. As much as she hated her job, she knew that Mr. Anderson was wrong. She massaged the back of her neck to ease some tension and held a deep breath in. There was just no way around this; she couldn't grant him coverage just because there was a clerical error.

"Mr. Anderson, I'm not giving you the run-around. I'm giving you the correct information. The insurance is paid by your employer, not by you. The specialist denied coverage because you went into the water on your own accord while you were off the clock. You decided to jump into the water and had an unfortunate encounter with a bull shark."

His voice deepened with rage. "Do you know what the shark did to me? It bit my right hand off!"

"Well technically, it bit off three of your fingers, but the hospital was able to reattach two." *Fuck! Why did I say that?*

"Not my middle finger," he screamed, "which I wish I had ready if I ever saw you!"

Oh Lord, here we go! Diana cleared her throat nervously, "I'm very sorry that you experienced this traumatic event. Despite what Gwen had advised you, she has no authority over a specialist and, therefore, we cannot grant you coverage."

There was a long pause before the shit hit the fan. Mr. Anderson absorbed her words and then he yelled at the top of his lungs.

"You fucking cunt! You *will* give me my money and I *will* get you fired!"

Thank God! I can finally end this! After she heard the next curse word, she quickly spoke over him. "Sir, you have been warned about using profanity. I am now disconnecting the call. Goodbye!"

She disconnected the call and notated the file so she could escape his claim. *I do not want to be locked into this when he calls back.* She could feel her heart pounding in her ears and sweat trickling down her back. Diana wrote down the claim number and shot her boss an email about the conversation. Normally, an employee could be terminated if they disconnected a call, but Diana had a legitimate excuse. It was the only excuse her work permitted.

"I don't get paid enough for this crap," she muttered.

She hated sending feedback forms to her boss involving another co-worker, especially Gwenyth, but this was a serious error that needed to be corrected. Unfortunately, it wasn't the first, second, or tenth time that she had to notify her boss of her coworker's mistakes. Diana had no ill feelings toward Gwenyth. She just had to cover her own ass.

In all honesty, she secretly admired her beauty and wished that they were friends, but Diana was too shy to start up a conversation. Gwenyth was practically a runway model with double Ds. She had luminous, blemish-free skin, and her hair was the prettiest shade of auburn. Diana only knew how to straighten her dark wavy hair and how to put concealer on her porcelain skin. The one time she applied purple eyeshadow, Tom nearly threw a fit and said she looked like a clown. She just wanted to enhance her Irish green eyes, but he convinced her that the beauty consultant only wanted to make a sale.

Work had a relaxed dress code, which was the only thing Diana loved about Sail-Co. Her idea of work clothes was yoga pants, racer-back tees, and a sweatshirt, where Gwenyth wore knit dresses that accentuated her tiny waist and curvy hips. Even her high heels made the sexiest clacking sounds down the hall. Diana sighed as she looked down at her beat-up sneakers. *It's too much work.*

After her standard shift hours of hell and an additional four hours of overtime, it was six in the morning. Diana was free . . . well, until it was six o'clock again. She heard her phone chime from her purse. It was a text message from Jordan, her bestie.

> **Jordan:** Bitch, it's game time! Will meet you at the parking lot! Don't be late again!

> **Diana:** Will be there in 10 minutes!

> **Jordan:** Don't be late!

Luckily, she had left her duffle bag in the back seat of her car. She almost forgot that she agreed to meet Jordan at the gym that morning. Diana ran down the stairs to the underground parking garage. Jordan was known for her punctuality. Death was the only excuse to be late. The last time Diana was late, their rep and set counts doubled. The gym was across the street, but she did not want to take any chances on leg day. She hurriedly threw her stuff in the car and peeled out of the parking lot.

Chapter 2

Diana and Jordan's friendship got off to an awkward start four years ago at their local gym. No matter what time Diana scanned herself in, she couldn't avoid that annoying gym creeper who would hover over her and tell her she was doing her workouts incorrectly. What bothered her the most was the fact that he was extremely overweight and he always went straight to her. She didn't consider herself experienced in bodybuilding, but she had taken enough boot camp classes to figure out what worked for her.

If he wasn't critiquing her form, he would find her and try to catch her attention by flexing and grunting inappropriately. She couldn't think of anything brilliant to say back, not even a simple "Don't bother me" or "Fuck off." Confrontation was not her strong suit. She was thinking about switching gyms since the front desk and the manager couldn't do much about him. They all called him by his secret nickname, Creep Show. She would never forget the day she last saw him. It was the day she met Jordan. Diana was doing her weighted squats on the Smith machine when he approached her again. His phlegmy smoker's voice made her skin crawl.

"You're not spreading your legs wide enough, and your butt needs to stick out more," he proclaimed. "Here, let me show you."

He was about to put his hand on her lower back when she recoiled from his grasp. Her face turned red as she cringed with disgust. Diana hooked the barbell behind her shoulders and grabbed her duffle bag from the corner. She was about to leave when she heard another voice that kept her rooted to the spot. A woman's voice echoed across the room with such tenacity.

"Hey, jerk!"

Diana turned her head and saw the woman behind the voice emerge from the cardio room. She radiated strength and beauty, standing slightly taller and with the physique of a bodybuilding champion. Her cocoa skin glowed with a captivating allure, complemented by hair that shimmered like gold. She appeared to be around Diana's age, embodying a powerful and striking presence. The man took a couple steps back as Jordan stared down at him with her intimidating, violet-blue eyes. Who would dare to oppose such a fierce goddess? Diana stood there in complete silence.

Jordan's brows narrowed as she crossed her arms in front of her. "Instead of running your mouth and harassing this girl, why don't you run your ass on the tread and then eat another donut?"

He stuttered. "I w-was only trying to—"

She tilted her head to the side and scrunched the bridge of her nose. "Leave? Good idea!"

Jordan's devilish smirk made him take off. Diana was astonished by what had just happened. *Rescued by a stranger . . . more like an angel.*

She snapped out of it when Jordan turned her attention to her. Her voice softened with a small chuckle. "Sorry, girl. I had to say something."

"No! Please don't apologize," Diana nervously giggled. "Seriously, thank you so much for helping me! I was ready to leave and never come back."

"Hah," her radiant smile lit up the room. "Well then, I'm glad that you didn't."

Diana blushed. *She is so stunning. Is that glitter on her or sweat? I can't tell.*

Jordan's sharp voice jolted her from her daze. "I was actually waiting for you to crack. I saw it in your face. You must be the strong, silent type."

Diana scratched the back of her head and giggled again, "No, not really. More like the cowardly and reserved type. It seriously takes me an hour to think of something good after the fact, and then when the time comes again, I'll never say it."

Jordan tilted her head and grinned. "Aww, you just need some practice. If they have the balls to harass you, then you should be allowed to do the same. It's fun. You should give it a try."

"You may be right about that." Diana's awkward giggling lessened. "So, umm . . . you look amazing. Do you do those competitions?"

"When I was younger, I got into bikini competitions, but now I just really do this for myself."

Diana was envious of her gorgeous, toned body. *It must have taken her years to look this perfect.* "Wow! Well, I'm very impressed! You look amazing."

She winked as she waved a pointed finger at her. "As do you. Don't let anyone tell you otherwise."

Her words gave Diana hope, but she didn't mean to make it so obvious. "Really?" she squealed.

"Absolutely! My name is Jordan, by the way. If you ever want to work out together, let me know."

Diana's eyes lit up. "That would be awesome!"

Since that day, they had built more than just muscles together. They became fit buddies for life, and Creep Show never bothered Diana again.

***

Diana easily spotted Jordan's new Range Rover. She was so proud of her best friend's most recent accomplishments. She made partner at her law firm, which was one of the largest and most established in the nation. Representing professional male athletes was Jordan's specialty, but sports in general were her strong suit. The best part of her job was access to season tickets for any upcoming soccer, basketball, or football games. Minnesota was their favorite place to explore, but they were mostly looking forward to their next trip in Jordan's new ride.

Diana parked right across from her as she saw Jordan opening her rear door. She was trying to pull on what looked like a leash.

"Come on, you little turd nugget!"

A tiny bark answered back. *She brought Bandit with her!*

Bandit was her new puppy, half-Siberian Husky and half-German Shepherd. She traveled all the way to Greenville this past Thanksgiving to pick him up from a farm at barely three months old. He finally jumped out of his seat sporting his "Service in Training" harness. Jordan was advised by her therapist that a furry companion could positively impact her health. *No one is perfect, even if they look it.*

She swung her gym bag over her shoulder and then hoisted Bandit with her other arm. Diana immediately ran up to pet the little guy.

"Aww! Handsome Bandit baby! I could just eat you up. Look at those big puppy eyes. You are just *so* fluffy!"

Jordan laughed. "I knew you were going to do this."

Diana scratched him behind his big floppy ears as he panted. "I seriously can't help it! He's so stinkin' cute!"

Jordan smiled. "The gym owner said it was okay to bring him along."

Diana had always wanted a dog, but Tom told her it was out of the question. His idea of a pet was a rock. She looked up at her friend with happy tears forming. "This is seriously making my day."

After a couple hours of what Jordan liked to call "kicking ass's ass," they sat in the nearby café for their usual breakfast of eggs Florentine with tomatoes. Bandit was tied to the base of their table, where he rested his head on his paws and looked up at them with pleading eyes. Jordan stirred her coffee and raised her eyebrows, waiting for Diana to spill more details about the surprise dinner that she made for Tom.

"So besides dealing with Mr. Anderson and all the other loonies, how was the rest of your day? Did Tom enjoy his meal?"

Diana sighed. "He was studying, so I didn't get the chance to see him before work. I did make the table look nice, though."

Jordan rested her chin on her palm and stared at her with discontent. "So, let me see if I got this right: He wasn't there when you came back from work. He wasn't there after you woke up. And then he wasn't there before you left for work again?"

"Well . . ." She hesitated and then cleared her throat. Her leg started to bounce. "He told me that he really needed to focus on his studying. He doesn't want to take the test for the third time, you know? I promised him that I would just get out of his way."

Jordan rolled her eyes and then returned her gaze with a hint of aggravation. "Oh, I remember!"

"Please don't give me that look," Diana begged.

Jordan took a slow sip from her cup and stared at Diana as if she was going to stage an intervention. "You know how I feel about him. How can you be with someone who throws temper tantrums, who blames you for his failures, and who constantly makes you feel like garbage? He's a gigantic asshole."

"Jordan," Diana pleaded.

But she persisted. "Please don't tell me he's been gone for nearly two days just to 'study.' His second test is in February. You realize that it is in two and a half months? It's obvious that he's full of shit."

Diana took a deep breath, then looked down at her napkin and nervously folded it over her lap. She could feel the stinging in her eyes as tears formed. She caught the hurt in her voice before it gave her away.

"He's just under a lot of pressure," she murmured. "I know that people don't act like themselves when they're stressed out. I'm just trying to be supportive. He's not that mean to me. I just overreact and get emotional sometimes."

"I understand pressure. Don't forget, I took the Bar Exam too," Jordan advised. "There's just something that isn't adding up, and I know you're smart enough to realize that he's not just studying." She set her cup down as she stared deeply into its blackness. "I can't stand the way he acts and the way he treats you—"

Diana shook her head as her tears got the better of her. "I don't want to talk about this anymore."

Jordan extended her hand across the table to cover Diana's and spoke in a softer tone. "I'm sorry that I upset you. I just want you to know that I say these things because I care. If there's something wrong—if he's not treating you right—I need you to tell me so I can help you."

Diana's brows furrowed as she bit her bottom lip. "Can we please change the subject?"

Jordan sighed. "Of course we can. . . So, I need to ask you a huge, last-minute favor."

Diana wiped her tears and nodded.

"Last night, I received a call to fly to Dallas for a client. It's only for this weekend. I can't really talk about it. It's highly confidential."

"Oh," Diana murmured.

"Yeah. The issue is I'll need to leave later today and I'll be flying back home on Sunday. The firm will not allow me to bring Bandit with me because he is not certified yet. My friends with dogs are also out of town, and I don't know anyone else who I can trust."

Diana so badly wanted to help, but knew that Tom was going to throw a fit if she took Bandit in. She looked down and stared into Bandit's icy blue eyes. His humongous shepherd ears made him look even more adorable. *Who could resist such a cute, innocent creature?* She frowned at the thought of him being alone.

"I understand that Tom will bitch if you take Bandit in," Jordan said. "So, I was wondering if I could give you a key to my house and you could house-sit."

Diana's eyes lit up.

"I will also pay you, as this is a lot to ask for in such short notice." Jordan pulled out her wallet from her bag. "I know that you and Tom want to spend your weekends together as well."

Diana shook her head. "I will definitely watch him, and there is no way that I'm going to let you pay me!"

"Nonsense." Jordan looked up from the cash she was pulling out. "I need to pay you."

"Absolutely not!"

Jordan laughed. "Well at least let me pay for breakfast!"

"That's fine," Diana giggled.

"And," Jordan rolled her eyes and smiled, "you can eat all my food and wear my clothes."

Diana cheered. "Deal!"

Chapter 3

They parted ways after breakfast. Jordan had to hurry home to make sure she was prepared for her trip. She planned to clean the house, place her key under her doormat and, of course, leave the TV on for Bandit.

Diana's home was just fifteen minutes away from the café, yet she felt a sense of urgency as she made her way there. The anticipation of seeing Tom was mixed with a hint of anxiety as she wondered about what awaited her. She bit the side of her tongue. She couldn't help but think about her discussion with her friend. *Jordan did bring up a good point. Two days does not make any sense to me either. I would have to be a fool to believe that he's been studying all this time, right? Then again...*

She didn't want to overthink it. She told herself she had the tendency of jumping to crazy conclusions, and she didn't want to start another fight with him.

Diana made it home and found a parking spot right away. After all, normal people with normal jobs were gone for work. Her timing was always fortunate on weekdays, as she avoided the usual struggle that comes with searching for a spot during peak hours. Before she stepped out, she quickly checked her reflection in the rearview mirror. Her makeup was slightly smeared under her eyes, so she rubbed most of it off with her fingers and patted down some of her flyaways. She smiled at herself and spoke in a tone that belied the hopeless look in her eyes. "Nothing a shower can't fix."

She rushed to her apartment, key in hand. As soon as she walked in, she stopped, the door slowly closing behind her. Tom was stuffing things into his backpack on the kitchen table. His blond hair was neatly combed. He had put on his best trousers and a blue dress shirt that she had only seen him wear once, to his cousin's wedding. She couldn't help but appear puzzled.

He glared at her with his dark brown eyes. "I don't have time to talk. I need to go."

She took a single step forward and lightly bit her knuckle before she spoke. *How can I ask him where he's going without sounding "pathetic?"* There was just no way around it.

"Well . . . I miss you. You look really nice today."

Tom rolled his eyes. "I got home three hours ago. If you made it home on time instead of working out with that ball-busting twit, I would have been able to better explain my situation to you."

His tone was more resentful than usual. Hearing him slander her friend was something she was trying to ignore. It always seemed that he enjoyed fueling his own anger by provoking her. If she gave him the reaction he was looking for, he would have the perfect excuse to unleash his sadistic rage on her. He would yell until she burst into tears and then yell louder about her crying. She could see a change come over him—like he was going in for the kill. To keep the peace, she had to think carefully about what to say next and to be mindful of her tone. Apologizing seemed to be the only way to diffuse the situation.

"I'm so sorry, Tom. I forgot I made a promise to Jordan."

"A promise?" he jeered. "To what, exactly? To look like a troll? Believe me, it's not attractive."

Her eyes began to tear up. *No! He can't say that to me and get away with it.* She bit her tongue before answering. Her voice rattled, but she got the words out. "Working out makes me feel better about myself."

He shook his head and then scoffed. "Pathetic."

"W-what do you mean?" she stuttered.

"You heard me." He zipped up his bag and then swung it over his shoulder.

"Tom, I know that you're still upset with me, and I'm really sorry, okay? What more can I do to make this right?"

He stared at her coldly as he approached. His voice deepened before her eyes veered to the floor.

"You can start by getting out of my way."

Diana looked behind her and realized she was blocking the doorway. She didn't want to move, but knew it was the most sensible thing to do. Her body froze as her mind was overwhelmed with conflicting emotions. Despite everything, she still loved him and wanted to mend whatever was broken. She wanted to fight for their relationship. She looked up at him with the little courage she had.

"No, I can't," she muttered.

"What?" His voice rose. "Use your words!"

"I don't want you to leave," she sobbed.

"Don't you dare start," he warned. "I'm sick of this!"

"We used to be so happy," she cried. "I don't know what's going on! You need to tell me so I can fix this!"

Before she knew it, he firmly grabbed her by the arms and flung her out of his way. She gasped as she felt the corner of the counter jab her hip. He stepped forward and his hands started to come up as if he was going to help her, but then he stopped. Diana looked up at him with tears running down her face. She held on to her hip as he sighed deeply.

"Diana, I don't have time for this."

She opened her mouth to speak, but no sound came out.

His hand reached for the door. "You and I will need to have a discussion when we're both home."

As he turned his back to her, she quickly remembered the other promise that she had made to Jordan.

"Tom," she whimpered.

Still facing the door, he grunted as he twisted the knob, "What?"

"I want us to work this out, but I need you to know that I have to house-sit this weekend, so I won't be home for a bit."

"Let me guess, Jordan wants you to watch that mutt of hers?"

She stared down and nodded with sudden regret.

"For how long? Is she even going to pay you?"

She sniffled. "Well, I'm not letting her. It's only for this weekend."

He shook his head. His grating voice persisted. "That's what I thought. Well, I don't care what you do. We need some time apart from each other anyway."

He wants more time away from me? Diana put her hands together, as if in prayer. "Tom, I will see you tomorrow. I promise."

"You better not bring that mangy animal here."

He slammed the door and left her alone again. Diana pressed her back against the wall and slid down to the tile floor. She wrapped her arms around her knees and broke down. She didn't know what she had done to set him off. *He wasn't always like this. This started way before his test, but when? He never hated animals, especially puppies! How can stress change someone so drastically? Or is it me who has changed?*

She tried to focus on all the good memories she had with him. She remembered their time as high school sweethearts and how he would always protect her from pranks. She remembered how he would hold her close while they were riding his bike down the neighborhood trail and how he would rescue her from her home when her parents had intense arguments. She remembered how he shaved his head after she got a bad haircut before their homecoming dance. She remembered when they shared their first kiss and when she gave herself completely to him. He was her first and only "everything."

She didn't realize that an hour had passed until her phone notified her of a new text message. She pulled her phone out of her pocket after wiping her tears with the back of her hands.

Jordan: *Off to the airport!*

Diana: *Be safe!*

Diana slowly picked herself off the floor. An intense, stabbing pain throbbed from her hip. She could feel it spread all the way down to her bottom.

She pulled at the elastic band of her pants to inspect the injury. There was already discoloration. *This would have never happened if I had gotten out of his way . . . and who seriously designed this stupid kitchen?* Her eyes then veered to the table. *He didn't even touch his meal.*

After clearing the table and washing the dishes, she found herself debating whether to throw out the dessert. A huge slice had already been eaten. A small part of her wanted to laugh. *So, he had time to eat some of this? Interesting.*

Her leisurely plans for the day involved a brief visit to Jordan's house. After a quick shower and packing essentials, she aimed to relax, play with Bandit, maybe catch a nap, before heading to work. She was trying to decide if taking a half-day would help her gather her thoughts before seeing Tom again. She didn't know what they were going to discuss, but her gut was telling her that it wasn't going to be anything good.

Are we breaking up? No. Whatever happens, I'll change. I'll do whatever it takes.

Chapter 4

Diana clocked in to begin her next shift. She sluggishly made it to her desk and dropped into her seat. She had settled into Jordan's house, but she wasn't able to sleep—not after what happened with Tom. Having a good cry was the only way to help her feel numb, especially on the drive up. Her eyes were burning slightly, and she knew that her eyelids had to be puffy with all the wailing she had done. She typed a few hollow clacks to log on and then scoffed when she saw the lagging on her screen. Once again, her computer was not cooperating. She pressed both of her palms against her tired eyes and took a deep breath.

A familiar giggle made her drop her hands. Diana peeked over her cubicle wall. It was Gwenyth, beautiful as ever. She had replaced last week's flowers with a new bouquet of pink roses. Their delicate hue matched her dress. She showed off the attached handwritten card to her friends. A part of Diana wanted to roll her eyes, but she knew that deep down she was just envious. *Gwen must have a special person—or multiple suitors—in her life to give her gifts every week, but beautiful people typically have it way easier.*

Diana looked at herself with disappointment. The black sleeves of her jacket held what was left of her concealer along with an unknown crust. *Maybe I have really let myself go and that's why he can't stand me.*

She had an idea. *Maybe I could learn a couple tips and tricks to get my relationship back on track.* She got up from her seat and gave her tired eyes one final rub without realizing that her mascara was smeared all over her face. She tried putting on a smile to look somewhat approachable and walked up to Gwenyth's cubicle. When her friends saw Diana, their faces motioned for Gwenyth to turn around.

"Well hello there, stranger," she smiled.

Diana smiled back. "Hello, Gwen. Those are some beautiful flowers you got there."

"I know, right? They're from my boyfriend."

"Wow, boyfriend," Diana exaggerated. "That's so sweet! How long have you been together?"

She giggled. "Well, I would have to say off and on for about a year."

"Oh?" She couldn't believe that even Gwenyth didn't have the most perfect relationship.

"Well," she continued, "we have a very passionate relationship, but I have the feeling he's more committed this time. He's definitely showing progress toward what I want in a man."

Diana smiled in astonishment. "Wow, so it's like you have him wrapped around your finger?"

Gwenyth smirked as she held a mirror to her face while applying her luscious red lipstick. "Let's just say he has a few things that he needs to sort out and then he will be."

Diana chuckled. "I need to know how you do it."

Her eyes lit up with curiosity. "Do what, exactly?"

"This!" Diana waved her hand in a circular motion in front of her.

Gwenyth laughed and nodded with appreciation.

"I mean, how are you so well put together and how do you have so much control in your relationship?"

She smirked once more and then looked down at Diana. "Do you really want my advice? I have the tendency of being very blunt."

Diana nodded with desperation. She needed all the help she could get.

Suddenly, a sharp voice interrupted their conversation. "Miss Diana Quinn, I need to speak with you in my office immediately," Brenda called, pointing the way as if Diana wasn't already familiar. She followed her boss with her head down.

What did I do this time? It's always something!

Behind her, Gwenyth shrugged her shoulders and giggled. Her friends flocked back to the edge of her cubicle and snickered at Diana's "raccoon eyes."

Brenda closed the door behind them and motioned for her to sit. She took out a box of tissues and handed it to her, although her tone was dull. "You have mascara smeared all over your face. You look like roadkill."

Diana was mortified. She immediately grabbed a few tissues and began wiping.

Brenda sounded exhausted. "It appears we're having computer issues again, aren't we?"

Diana bit her bottom lip. "I couldn't log in."

Her boss's annoyance was obvious. "So, asking Gwen about her personal life will fix that issue?"

Diana shook her head. "I just wanted to ask her a question. I—"

"From the looks of it, you're having a difficult time. If your computer is not working sufficiently and if you're not making your work time useful, I would highly suggest you go home for the day."

Diana wanted to argue, but she had been thinking about taking a half-day anyway.

"You don't look well, and I need to make an official complaint to HR regarding your lack of performance."

Her heart pounded with rage. "What are you saying? That I'm not performing to the best of my ability because I was asking Gwen a personal question?"

Brenda nodded with a devious smile.

Diana's eyes narrowed. "You never micromanage her when she's talking to her friends, which she's doing now, by the way."

Looking through the office window confirmed she was right, but her manager couldn't care less. She pursed her lips as Diana continued.

"You have never confronted her about her poor claim handling either. I'm always sending you feedback emails regarding the customer complaints."

Brenda crossed her arms and squinted her eyes. "Micromanage, you say?"

Diana grabbed another tissue and sobbed pathetically. "I've been here for over two years. I've never called in sick. I've always worked overtime and always sent you my tickets from technical support. I don't know what you have against me, but it isn't fair."

"You are the only employee who has complained about computer issues. Your metrics on call-handling times are atrocious. Meanwhile, Gwen gets her work done in a timely manner instead of dwelling on errors that were caused by other associates."

Diana tightly gripped her tissue and nearly shook out of anger. "So, what you're telling me is that the quality of the work doesn't matter anymore? That it's okay to make constant errors as long as I get in and out of the claim quickly?"

Brenda got out of her chair and responded with her usual calm yet conspiring smile. "Like I said, I highly suggest you take the day off. I will notify HR and we'll discuss this further on Monday."

Brenda waved her hand forward, signaling for her to leave. Diana got up from her seat and walked out without making further eye contact. She went to her cubicle, grabbed her purse, and scanned her ID card to clock out. The gossiping across from her was constant, but she kept moving. She just had to leave that hellhole.

Once she was in her car, she laughed at the state of her life. "Gee, I can't wait to see what tomorrow will bring."

Chapter 5

Diana hit the tail end of evening traffic, but eventually made it back to Jordan's in one piece. She needed to get some rest, as her vision began to blur and a headache was coming on.

When she finally opened the door, little Bandit galloped her way. She couldn't resist smiling at the pup. She hugged him and held him against her chest. He rested his head underneath her chin and looked up at her with such happiness. His affection was exactly what she needed. It was as if all her troubles disappeared within those few seconds. She gave him a small peck on the head before setting him free.

It was almost eight o'clock. She changed out of her work clothes and into her flannel pajamas. She went into the bathroom and, for the first time since leaving Jordan's house earlier, she saw her face in the mirror. It was horrible. Mascara was smeared around her eyes, her cheeks, her nose, and even on her forehead. It looked like she was developing a rash around her eyes from the constant rubbing. *Straight outta some horror film—a zombie one.*

After a short, sardonic laugh at her own expense, she washed her face and rummaged through Jordan's bathroom, where she found a soothing mask. She wanted to look somewhat normal for Tom. She read through the instructions as she secured her hair with a headband.

"Hmm . . . hydrating lavender? Maybe I'll get some good sleep, too." She shrugged her shoulders and plastered the cream all over her face.

As she walked into the kitchen, Bandit caught a glimpse of her purple face and barked in panic. He took refuge in his kennel and hid under his blanket. Half of his face poked out to see what she was going to do next.

She giggled. "Suit yourself, little guy."

Diana knew Jordan had a weakness for pumpkin pie gelato. She grabbed the last pint. "You're mine now, sucka."

After she settled herself on the couch, she turned on the TV, but couldn't find anything worth watching. She left the local weather channel on for background noise as she skimmed through her messages. She wasn't sure if Tom was home or if he was "studying." She didn't like how they left things and she wasn't sure if texting him was a good idea. Bandit slowly crawled out of his kennel and approached her. He stood up on his hind legs at the edge of the couch and whimpered for her attention. She sat him on her lap before she started texting.

> **Diana:** Hope your studying went well, and I hope you made it home safely. I wasn't feeling my best, so I took some time off from work. I'll probably sleep in.

Before she could eat another spoonful of gelato, she received a response. It was just a thumbs up emoji. Diana started to type that she loved and missed him, but she hesitated. Instead of hitting the Send button, she deleted her message. As she was about to set her phone down, she noticed that her screen showed he was typing. Her phone chimed.

Tom: I have work at eight, but I'll be home around two. What time should I expect you?

Diana bit the side of her bottom lip. She knew that she had to see him to work things out. Her heart raced at the thought of a potential break-up conversation. As before, she shut her eyes tightly and shook her head. *No, it can't happen.* She was ready to ask him whether they were over, but her phone notified her of another message first. Its length surprised her.

Tom: I know that things have been rough between us for some time. I realize now that I have played a part in that, but I know that in time, things will work out for the better. Even though you have to house-sit at Jordan's, can we at least meet up for a dinner date tomorrow night? We can go to that steakhouse that you've always wanted to try.

She was trying to reassure herself that things just might turn around. Maybe he felt bad about throwing her against the counter? Maybe he was going to apologize. She cracked a small smile and began typing. She knew that she had to get a good night's rest and then later she could sneak back into their apartment for a cute outfit and makeup for their date night.

Diana: If it's okay with you, can we meet up at 4pm?

Tom: Absolutely! 4 actually works better for me! I'll have a table reserved for us. Make sure you get plenty of rest tonight and tomorrow morning. Love you.

Diana: I love you too. Goodnight.

That next morning, Jordan's alarm clock went off with an incredible *BANG!* Diana clambered out of bed as fast as she could. Still trying to open her eyes, she screamed when she stepped on something furry and heard Bandit's yelp. She couldn't see anything, but she felt her heart pounding as a masculine voice kept yelling. Her ears finally registered a trumpet playing *Reveille*, the Army's wake-up call.

"Wake your ass up! Get up! Get your damn ass out of bed! This ain't your mama!"

A second later, Diana realized it was the voice of one of Jordan's favorite fitness influencers. What a lovely prank her friend had played on her. She turned it off and laughed before texting her friend.

Diana: *Wow! I gotta get me one of those alarms!*

Jordan: *Bahahaha! I'm glad you loved it. #SorryNotSorry*

Diana shook her head and then turned to Bandit. "Your mama is one crazy lady."

She couldn't go back to bed. She had to get her day started, especially if Tom was already at work. As the coffee brewed, she let Bandit out. She was surprised by how dark the sky was. It was still pretty early for snow, but with Midwest weather, you could never really tell. It was definitely chilly out. Diana wrapped her arms around herself and stared at Bandit, who was gnawing on a stick.

"Hurry up and pee!"

When they finally went back inside, she picked up the TV remote to turn on the weather channel. Heavy rains and thunderstorms were in the forecast.

After she drank her coffee, she hopped into the shower while blasting Jordan's speaker. *Today is gonna be a good day! Things will turn around. I just know it!* Knowing there was nobody around to complain, she sang as loud as she could and failed miserably to stay on-key. She laughed as she attempted to match her voice to the greatest pop singers of all time. She didn't even come close. As she was rinsing the shampoo out of her hair, she heard a big *KABOOM*! Suddenly, the speaker and all the lights shut off. Bandit yelped down the hall.

Great. . . . Now I can't see.

She turned the knob before another loud bang startled her. Then, heavy rain followed. *This is seriously happening now?* Diana rolled her eyes and grunted with annoyance. She put on Jordan's robe and wrapped a towel around her head. All the lights were off, and the living room ceiling fan was slowly spinning to its end. A small amount of daylight peeked through the blinds and curtains. She walked to the nearest window to confirm her suspicions. *Oh, it's definitely happening. I seriously hope this doesn't ruin our night.*

She clumsily got ready, then grabbed her purse and keys. As the thunder progressed, she heard Bandit whimper from the corner of the room. Diana did not want to leave him in the house by himself. She figured that it wouldn't do any harm if she brought him. If the storm cleared a little, they could go out for a walk. *Tom should be at work by now. He won't find out.*

"All right, you little cutie." She clipped the leash on his harness. "We're going out."

They ran as fast as they could down the driveway. *And of course, I left my umbrella at the apartment! God, I'm dumb.*

Bandit got comfortable in the back seat as she started her car. As he shook the water off, Diana instantly regretted not bringing a towel for him. "It's fine! We're going!"

It appeared the power outage had affected most of the area. Police officers directed vehicles while the streetlights flashed red at every intersection. There were a few minor accidents on the way that made traffic even more congested. Luckily, they lived in the city, where hazards would be managed promptly. With the thunder rumbling almost constantly, Diana needed a distraction. She held her finger on the radio's Scan button to find a station with a clearer frequency. "Nothing? Wow."

Their complex had more residents than parking spaces. On weekdays, the lot was nearly empty. On weekends, she was never home at the right time to find a space close to her apartment. *Of course, the lot is full. Nobody wants to be out in this mess!* She parallel-parked across the street, where there were some office buildings and a café that she and Tom used to visit.

She exhaled deeply before she spoke to Bandit. "This is gonna be quick. I promise!"

She braced herself before walking through the downpour, but it did not make much of a difference. The rain spat at her ferociously, like bullets. The cold winds blew through her hair, entangling and frizzing it all over again. Within seconds, she was drenched. She closed the car door behind her and wrapped her arms around herself, glancing up at the dark sky.

That's not good. It's like a bad omen . . .

She took a few steps forward, but halted when she heard Bandit howling from the back seat. He looked at her through the rear window with his sad puppy eyes. Raging thunder snapped in the distance, loud enough to make her flinch. Feeling guilty about leaving him alone, she assured herself that Tom wasn't there. She opened the back door and grabbed his leash.

"All right, come on. But no nonsense!" Bandit yipped in response. They ran as fast as they could through the storm.

Diana allowed Bandit to give himself one last shake before she opened the apartment door. She peeked inside before walking in and quietly shut the door behind them. The kitchen and living room were dark, but it seemed a few candles were still lit on the table. She rushed over to blow them out. *How could Tom forget? Does he want to burn the place down?*

She opened the blinds to let some light in, but then heard a massive *THUMP* come from their bedroom. Bandit ran to follow the noise, but she got ahold of him.

Her heart jumped. *He's not at work? Oh, God! That's all I need—another fight!*

She did not want to risk it. As she was about to pick up Bandit and sneak out, she heard another *THUMP* followed by two people laughing. She recognized Tom's voice, but couldn't seem to make out the other. Then, she heard a woman giggling.

Bandit dragged her to the bedroom door, which was slightly open. Candlelight flickered from their room. She was reluctant to open it further, but knew she had to.

Without her realizing it, Bandit pushed the door open with his front paws. *No!* Her heart sank when she found Tom caressing another woman beneath him—in their sheets. A high-pitched bark caught their attention. The woman instinctively shielded her nude body with a pillow, then lifted her head above it. Diana was stupefied by her smug, yet familiar expression.

"Gwenyth!"

Tom, on the other hand, was not as surprised to see her, although his face contorted with rage as he made his way out of the bed. Instead of coming up with an explanation or a lie, he chose to say nothing. He grabbed his clothes from the side of the bed and started to dress himself.

Candles were lit all over their dresser. Every single one of her hidden romance novels were exposed and dumped all over the floor. Diana froze, choking back tears. She did not know what to do or say, so she began stuttering.

"M-my books. Why—"

Tom eyed her with disgust. "Why are you here?"

Diana was stunned. *This is wrong! This is so wrong! Say something, Diana!* How could there be no signs of sympathy, regret, or mortification? It was as if he was a completely different person. Or was this, in fact, the real him?

"Why am *I* here?" Diana nearly choked on her words. "How can you ask me that? I live here! How could you do this to, to us?"

Gwenyth laughed playfully. "Well, isn't this is just grand?"

Diana's voice grew louder. "You think this is funny?"

Tom stepped in front of her before she could even approach the homewrecker. "Diana, you need to calm down!"

"What?"

He glared at her. "You weren't supposed to be here. You were supposed to meet me later tonight!"

"Gee, sorry I ruined your plans," she replied sarcastically. "How long were you gonna keep this a secret?"

He threw on his shirt and started buttoning it. "I was going to officially end it with you tonight."

"Our last date? Oh, how romantic of you." Her voice shook as tears ran down her cheeks. "So last night, when you texted me that you loved me, you lied! You lied to me this entire time! You're a liar and a coward!"

Tom grabbed her by the collar with both of his hands and pushed her against the wall. His knuckles dug deep into her chest. The pressure made it difficult to breathe. Instinctively, she turned her face away from his, but that enabled him to scream into her ear. She winced in pain as he pressed deeper.

"Coming from a person who pretends that everything is fine! Someone who is completely spineless!"

"Tom, stop! You're hurting me!"

He shouted over her. "You need to hear the truth in person! We fell out of love a long time ago! It's over! I want you out!"

Tears clouded her vision as her body quivered in his grasp. Bandit squeezed between their feet and barked at Tom aggressively. That, of course, came to an end the second he gave the puppy a vicious look. Bandit hid behind Diana's legs and whimpered with fear. Tom's attention turned back to her. He stared down at her with his cold eyes.

"You never listen to me. You even brought that filthy animal here after I told you not to!"

He gave her one last shove before he let go and backed up to the foot of the bed. He had to step away to compose himself. Gwenyth smirked from behind him and wrapped her bony arms around his neck. She was enjoying every second of this. Diana picked Bandit up off the floor and held him close to her aching chest.

"He's not a filthy animal, Tom. You are." She turned to face the door and spoke once more. "I'll come back in a couple of days to get my things."

He scoffed before her hand touched the knob. He wanted to have the last word. "By the way, you *suck* in bed."

Diana froze. She knew that she needed to leave as his belittlement continued on.

"Yeah, that's the honest truth, if you ever wanted to know why I cheated in the first place. One of the lousiest lays of my life!"

Gwenyth laughed and chucked one of the romance novels at her back. "Here! Use this for more inspiration."

Diana ran out of the apartment, crying hysterically. She had never felt so humiliated and unloved in her life. The rain grew into a torrent. Back inside the Versa, she sat behind the wheel and wept. Bandit snuggled in her lap, doing his best to comfort her.

She couldn't believe that their eight-year relationship had ended like that, as if it was nothing to begin with. And out of all the people he could cheat with, it had to be the coworker she envied. *What are the odds? How did they meet? How long have they been together?*

Beethoven's *Symphony No. 5* startled her. Between her sobs, she managed to pull her phone out of her back pocket and hit the End Call button before she went back to wailing. *Not now!* Talking to her mother then wouldn't have helped in the least.

Suddenly, Diana heard a couple of hard knocks on her driver's-side window. She jumped and screamed with fear. The heavy rain made it difficult to see the stranger on the other side.

"Excuse me, miss," he yelled out over the storm. "Are you okay?"

Bandit barked back. Diana freaked out and kept dropping the keys in her lap. As soon as she steadied her hand, she started her car and drove off. The stranger was left on the side of the road, completely drenched.

Chapter 6

The car shook as the winds blew harder. The clouds wept heavily, and the streets began to flood. What was next? Massive hail the size of golf balls? Or better yet, a tornado? Diana relished the thought of being blown away. The sky darkened and lightning struck all around her. As the thunder rumbled and rattled the earth, she saw the town's power go out again. It caused chaos as traffic came to a standstill at every intersection. The lack of streetlights left drivers confused, further adding to the already tense situation.

She needed to get off the street. It was difficult to concentrate on the road with what she just discovered. She looked around for the nearest exit and found one small building that still had functioning lights. After pulling into a parking spot, she turned off her vehicle and pressed her forehead against the steering wheel. She shut her eyes tightly and prayed with everything she had that she would *not* cry again. Every time she tried taking a deep breath, she felt her lungs tightening. She thought she was going to lose her mind. The last panic attack she had was in college when she was preparing for finals. Before her fit could take hold, the rain suddenly stopped. She heard nothing, not even a gust of wind.

Distracted by the unnatural silence, she raised her head from the steering wheel and looked at her surroundings. She noticed the glowing sign on the building in front of her. It was a bookstore that was literally called A BookStore. It had to be new; otherwise, she would have already known about it. It didn't seem new, though, based on its haunting appearance. Its sage green siding was warped, and the white chipping paint of the door with its hazy window created an air of mystery. The parking lot was covered with potholes, but that was Michigan in general. Oddly enough, she was the only one there. *Perhaps it's not open yet?*

Bandit climbed on her lap and licked her face, which jolted her back to reality.

"Oh, hey buddy!" she said and turned to scratch him behind his ears. "Guess you want to go outside, huh?"

He leaned into her hand and looked at her with his icy blue eyes. Diana sighed lovingly. "Okay, let's go."

Outside the car, Bandit took to loudly sniffing everything, which Diana didn't mind. She had nowhere to go until traffic cleared anyway. They both heard bells jingle as the door opened. A thin elderly woman stepped out to greet them.

"Oh, look at the both of you! Completely drenched! Come inside!" She appeared to be in her mid-sixties, with long silver ringlet curls and enough makeup to advertise an entire beauty line. She was dressed like a gypsy, and she even wore those ridiculously large golden hoop earrings. Diana was about to respectfully decline, but a loud crack in the sky couldn't stop her hand from rising to her chest. Bandit pulled at the leash and dragged her toward safety.

A BookStore was tiny, and it had a lot of unusual antiques. There was functional lighting in the ceiling, but numerous candles scattered about gave it a calming ambiance. Diana couldn't identify the familiar smell of the place, but it reminded her of her childhood visits to her Nona's house.

The store owner smiled as she handed her a towel. "It's frankincense and sage . . . they calm the spirits." She then wrapped a towel around Bandit and fed him a little jerky. Diana looked around and only saw four small bookcases. Every hardcover book had a warped shell. She couldn't identify any of them.

The lady stared at Diana with enthusiasm. "See anything you like, my dear?"

She replied with curiosity. "Is this . . . a bookstore?"

"I thought my sign had made that pretty clear," the old woman said with a chuckle.

Diana shook her head with sudden regret. "I'm so sorry. I didn't mean to offend you. I just see very few books in here—"

She cut her off with a sweep of her hand. "Amongst other things."

From her cleavage, she pulled out a pink satin handkerchief and wiped Diana's face. Diana tried not to cringe outwardly. *This old lady is trying to be nice. Calm down!*

The shop owner put her hands on Diana's cheeks and pulled her face closer. She looked deeply into her sad eyes, as if she was looking straight into her soul, then sighed with pity.

"My goodness, child. It appears that you had quite the day already."

"Uh-huh." She nodded as she looked down at her feet. *Don't say anything. Don't you dare start crying again and make a total ass of yourself.*

She bit her tongue to distract herself from her out-of-control emotions. Then all of a sudden, the lady that had shown such concern and kindness seconds earlier, gave her a hard slap across the face. Diana cupped her cheek and took a step back, staring at this woman that was apparently bat-shit crazy. Diana's cheek was throbbing, and the sound of the slap echoed in the store. Bandit just laid there without a care in the world. Diana felt her face turning red, but not from the pain.

"Ow! What's your deal, lady?"

The lady gleefully skipped behind the register and sang "What is Love?" by Haddaway. She obviously had a few screws loose.

"We are so outta here!" Diana said as she pulled Bandit by his leash toward the door.

"I have something for you, my dear," she whispered.

Diana paused. *What now?* "Umm sorry, but we need to leave."

"Just one more moment."

The lady bent over to open the cabinet door beneath the register and lifted out a heavy steel box secured by a gigantic golden padlock. She took a key from her skirt pocket and unlocked it. She pulled out what appeared to be an old book. Looking at its heft, it had to contain over a thousand pages. Its vintage brown leather cover was adorned with heart-shaped embellished corners. It had a gold-coated spine, and leather straps bound it shut.

The woman held the book against her chest and chanted an unusual lullaby. She embraced the book while she kept her eyes closed.

"Romanorum, passionis, ac libidinis librum tibi dono dabo. Donum verus amor."

The lady swayed with the beat of her song. Entranced by the performance, Diana was reminded of Sméagol's "precious" from *The Lord of the Rings*. As Diana's hand started to push on the door, the lady was suddenly there, blocking her exit. Before Diana could say or do anything, the lady placed the book in her hands. She wasn't sure what the shop owner was trying to sell, and she wasn't planning on finding out. She tried politely returning it.

"It's on the house, my dear. Please take it," she insisted as she shoved it back into her arms.

Diana gave her a concerned look. "Umm . . . I don't know."

The lady placed her hands over her hips with a raised brow. "Do you not know how to say thank you when receiving a gift?"

Diana drew back in shock. "Oh no, I'm so sorry! Thank you so much! What kind of book is this?"

The lady smiled and spoke in an oddly seductive tone. "It's a special book. Full of romance, adventure . . . and magic. It will take you to places that you have never been, even in your wildest dreams."

Diana laughed nervously. *She's completely off her rocker, but then again, who would refuse a free book? And how else am I supposed to get out of here?* Before she knew it, both of her cheeks were cupped again. Diana cringed and kept her eyes shut as she plotted her escape.

The lady whispered in her ear. "Go forth on your conquest of love." Within a second, she let go and slapped her again.

Diana rubbed her other cheek. "Ow!" she grunted. "Woman, just who do you think you are?"

"Go forth, my child!" she shouted. "Go forth and fulfill your desires!"

"Oh geez! Okay, fine! We're leaving!"

She scooped up Bandit and ran out the door. "Crazy old hag!"

The sky was still dark, but at least traffic had finally cleared. Once they made it to her car, she looked behind her to see the old lady watching her from the store window, cheering her on. "Oh God, Bandit! We need to go!"

Bandit climbed in the passenger seat while Diana threw the book behind her. It bounced off the seat and onto the floormat.

When she started her car, the radio played Haddaway. She screamed and quickly changed the station. She sped out of the parking lot with shivers running down her spine.

"Bandit, why does it feel like I've been cursed?"

Bandit barked in response. "Good idea! Let's get some booze!"

On the way back to Jordan's, Diana made a quick detour for her favorite drinks, pizza, and some booze-filled chocolates. At that point, the best plan of action seemed to be getting shit-faced. "What a day! Got cheated on and bitch-slapped twice!"

She tried calling Jordan a couple of times, but she was instantly directed to her voicemail.

Chapter 7

Her whole Saturday had been wasted. Diana made it back to Jordan's house safely, but the power was still out even after she tried messing with the electrical panel. She was aware of the potential hazards, but she didn't care. At least she thought ahead by drinking half a bottle of Jack Daniel's whiskey. She had the booze, the pizza, and the chocolates! If only the TV would turn itself on, she could watch the Bridget Jones trilogy to complete her night of misery.

It was getting late, and she wasn't sure when the storm was going to pass. Her phone rang again with Beethoven's blaring tune. Diana took a deep breath while she looked at the caller ID screen. *With fifteen percent left? Hell no.* She burped as she ended the call and tossed her phone onto the couch next to her.

There were no candles around, but all of Jordan's camping equipment was in her garage. She found five LED battery-operate camping lanterns. With success freshly obtained, Diana decided to camp out in the family room. In spite of her wobbly legs and her arms either losing all their strength or having too much strength, she managed to put together a nice fort for herself and Bandit with all the blankets and pillows from Jordan's room. She also knew that if she brought food into Jordan's bedroom or threw up all over her new Tempur-Pedic mattress, she would never be forgiven.

Being drunk and productive would keep her mind off of Tom and his new slut of a girlfriend, or so she thought. "I bet that skank isn't even a natural redhead," Diana slurred to herself, laughed, and then took another sip of regret.

She let her gaze wander around the room, trying to think of what else she could do to make the time pass faster. Her eyes then landed on the weird book she had brought in from the car.

"Hey Bandit, let's have a story night!" She snatched up the book and pretended she was the crazy old lady from the store. "Oh, my precious!"

She held the book close to her chest and started dancing. She immediately stopped when Bandit barked aggressively. "Geez! I thought it was funny."

She snorted and sat on the floor. "I didn't even catch her name. Did you?"

Bandit tilted his head with curiosity.

She set the bottle of Jack down beside her and undid the book's straps. She didn't know why, but she was in the habit of smelling books. She took one big whiff and chuckled. "You smell like frankincense and sage. Will you calm my spirit? We shall see."

She opened the book and hiccupped. The first page had a list of commandments.

Book Rules

    1. *Finish every chapter when expected.*

    2. *Follow the guiding lights.*

    3. *You are permitted bookmarks.*

4. You have one emergency escape. Choose wisely.

5. You have one wish.

6. Enjoy the pleasures that await you.

Diana laughed out of confusion. She'd never seen a book with rules to follow. She also didn't understand them. What were the "guiding lights" and how was she supposed to use "bookmarks" when the stupid book didn't come with them? She turned the page and read out loud.

Chapter 1: The Lady and the Raider

England, 1621 A.D.

It was a gloomy night. The clouds wept with sorrow as the moon hid its beauty. Lady Violet felt trapped in her own homestead and knew that she had to flee before sunrise. Confined and locked in her own quarters, she feared for tomorrow's events. She did not want to marry Lord Bennington, the Duke of Wellington. Lady Violet had been caught off guard when her mother, the countess, made arrangements for her marriage and began making demands of her.

"It is your duty as a lady of your status to marry Lord Bennington. Your father is no longer your guardian, and you will do as you are told. I shall not have my only daughter a spinster. You shall marry into a wealthy household and support the lot of us."

Lady Violet sobbed and tried to convince herself that her mother only wanted what was best for her and her family, their crops, and their servants. Their wealth had been dissipating. She wished her father had survived through the last fever. His word had power over the countess. Lady Violet held her candlestick close. Its small flame danced close to her bosom as if it was the only spirit that she had left. Lady Violet prayed for a miracle . . .

As Diana read, she felt a sudden knot in her stomach. She covered her mouth and looked down at her belly with regret. "I think I drank too much."

The lantern that she placed on the coffee table flickered rapidly, followed by one in the corner of the room. Diana shrugged. "Ooh, it must be the curse!" she chortled.

Bandit barked as she let out another hiccup. "Nah, my life can't be that fucked up."

It was at that moment that loud thunder rumbled across the sky. Diana flinched as Bandit jolted back into Jordan's room. "Haha. Nice!"

She took another gulp of Jack before she collapsed on her pillows. Her vision started to blur as she gazed at the ceiling. She closed her eyes and counted to ten. When she opened them, it appeared that the ceiling was spinning. Diana giggled as she sang "You Spin Me Round" by Dead or Alive.

The spinning intensified until her vision blurred completely. She closed her eyes again and was about to doze off when she felt a ferocious current of wind blow toward her. Adrenaline rushed through her body and her vison began to clear. Jordan's belongings were swept up by the powerful wind. It roared as it twisted her hair and clothing. She pressed her hands against her ears and closed her eyes again as she felt her body being lifted from the carpet.

"This is all just a nightmare." Bandit's barking echoing down the hall. "Or a tornado!"

Diana screamed at the top of her lungs until everything stopped. She was alone in the dark space, floating into the air . . . until her butt hit the floor.

"Ow!"

When Diana realized that she was stable again, she opened her eyes. Her vision spun as her head throbbed.

"And that, my friends, is the last time I'm drinking," she said to herself. "Seriously, Diana! Get your shit together!"

As her eyes cleared, she noticed a flickering candlestick lying on its side, illuminating a room with wooden floors. She instinctively picked up the candle, but she still couldn't make out where she was.

"I don't remember lighting any candles. Bandit?" She whistled, but she couldn't hear him. "Where the hell is he? Where the hell am I?"

She heard loud footsteps thudding toward the door to the room. Keys rattled from the other side, unlocking it aggressively. It opened with enough force to put a dent in the stone wall. Diana fell flat on her bottom again. When she looked up, she saw an older woman swinging a lantern above her head. Light flooded the room as she placed it on top of a nearby table.

The lady wore what appeared to be a dark red dress with a tight corset. It was too tight for her plump figure, and her breasts nearly touched her chin. Her ashy hair was put up in a bun. The lady stared down at Diana with her dark eyes. The way she grimaced reminded her of an evil cartoon villain ready to carry out her death sentence. Diana had bit her tongue to stifle a laugh, but she couldn't take her seriously. The lady snatched the candle from her hand while her hoarse voice rose.

"You can cause a ruckus all you want. You will no longer be my problem. Your carriage will arrive at any moment. I suggest you collect yourself."

As the lady was about to leave the room, she took a second glance at Diana and smirked once more.

"Violet, I had almost forgotten the gift that he left you as a token of his affection." She reached deep into her cleavage to pull out a golden locket. She playfully swung it above Diana's head and then dropped it on her lap. Diana picked herself off the floor while clasping it in her fist. She wrapped her arms around herself and then realized that she was not wearing her flannel pajamas anymore. *Strange dream. . . . Yeah, I must be dreaming.*

"My name is not Violet," she began to argue. "It is—"

The lady scoffed and left the room. She quickly slammed the door so Diana couldn't escape.

"Wait!" she ran to the door. "Don't lock me in here!"

She kicked the door as hard as she could, but it was too sturdy. She felt a jolt of pain up through her knee, and panic began to set in.

Diana grunted as she cupped her hand over her knee. "I'm gonna get out of here, and you'll be sorry."

She heard the old lady laughing down the hall. Diana tried to remain calm. She shut her eyes. "This is a dream . . . just a dream. Wake up!"

When she opened her eyes, she found herself in the same room. "Okay, so this is a nightmare."

She picked up the lantern the woman had left and walked around as if she was in one of those escape rooms, searching for clues.

"Resources. What are my resources?"

Her eyes roamed her surroundings. The wooden bedroom furniture had an antique style and golden trim.

"Okay, there's a bed with really gross sheets, a wardrobe . . . Crap. I'm in a haunted house."

When she looked up, she found what appeared to be a warped mirror. Diana gasped—she couldn't recognize her own reflection! She walked closer to get a better view. Her hair was no longer dark brown and wavy. It was now blonde with tight curls. Oddly enough, her eyes and face remained the same. Her clothes, on the other hand, were different. She wore a light blue dress with lace trim. She took notice of its corset and felt the tight pressure around her waist. As Diana started to realize what time period she was in, she couldn't hold back her laughter.

"Oh okay, I'm just in a drunken sleep! There's no way in hell that I'm a part—"

An intruding voice cut her off. Its deep, masculine tone sent a chill down her spine. "That you're a part of this story?"

Diana flinched as she held the lantern over her head. "Who said that?"

She looked around, but there was no one in the room.

"As I was saying," she gulped, "there's no way in hell that I'm a part of this . . . this—"

"Story!" The voice added.

Diana screamed and wrapped her arms around herself. "Show yourself, creep!"

He laughed. "You can't see me."

She screamed again. "Are you a ghost? I swear to God, if you are…"

"Technically, no. I'm just your narrator."

Diana looked up at the ceiling with confusion and shook her head with disbelief.

"Oh, yes I am," he teased. "If you want to get out of this chapter, you better do as I say."

She rolled her eyes and snorted. "You have the creepiest voice, man. Not gonna lie."

"Are you shitting me?"

Diana couldn't see him, but gave him a sour look. "I mean . . . my life is ridiculous enough as it is, but damn." She used her hand to cover her burp before she spoke again. "If a grim reaper could talk."

"My voice isn't that bad," he argued.

She chuckled. "Like how were you even chosen? If I could select someone to narrate my life, it would at least be someone who sounds a bit livelier . . . or comical. I should be able to choose, don't you think? Can I switch narrators?"

"Well, there's nothing that I can do. You're stuck with me." He laughed again. "I suppose that you can always wish for me to change my voice, but I don't want you to waste your one wish on a silly—"

"I fucking *wish* it!" Thunder roared and lightning struck over the roof as Diana shouted. "This is my damn dream!"

"You mean story," he replied.

"Whatever! Just do it!" Diana hiccupped. Like a brat, she placed her hands on her hips and stomped her foot on the hard wooden floor.

"Fine . . . yeesh!" His masculine tone rose slightly to sound more youthful, but he added a secret ingredient. "Does this satisfy you?"

Diana blushed. *Umm, that's sexy.* "Oh yeah . . . Now you can keep talking."

"Thank you."

"Wait!" She cut him off. "Do you have a name?"

"I don't," he responded, "but we seriously don't have enough time to chitchat. You, Lady Violet, will need to get your ass out of here before the duke arrives."

She snorted. "My name is Diana . . . and what's so bad about marrying this duke, huh?"

"Open the locket."

Diana opened the golden locket that had been given to her and saw a miniature image of an ugly old geezer.

"Oh shit. Okay! Hi, my name is Lady Violet," she yelled out with a forced smile. "How the hell do I get out of here?"

The Narrator took in a deep breath. "As this is the first chapter, I'm going to make it very easy for you. Just listen to me and do as I say. It will make the other chapters a breeze!"

Diana chucked the locket across the room as he continued speaking.

"See that window to your left? Open it and jump out."

Diana opened the window and saw she was on the second floor. "It's too high!"

"You need to trust me," he said. She didn't want to jump to conclusions, but she could have sworn he sounded annoyed.

She heard loud footsteps marching up the stairs. "Fine!"

Diana ran to the window and reached down at her sides to hike her dress up to her waist. She kicked one leg out the window and then the other until she was sitting on the ledge. Unable to see below her in the darkness, she pushed off the wall with her hands and feet. She let out a small scream and landed in a huge rose bush with thorns that dug into her skin. Tears spilled from her eyes as she gasped for air. *For a dream, this really hurts!*

As she was about to complain, The Narrator whispered for her to be quiet. She sunk further into the bush as she heard a man yell from Lady Violet's room.

"Guards, find that wench and bring her to me!"

"That's your cue!" The Narrator whispered sternly. "Run!"

Diana ran blindly until she found herself in the nearest town. She hid behind what looked like a brothel. Women in more revealing dresses laughed with their gentlemen companions. As her senses came back to her, she shivered and cupped her arms with her hands. The air smelled thick of salt and fish, and she could hear the loud cawing of seagulls. She noticed the sea, then a glowing green light flickering before her in the shape of an arrow. She remembered the second rule of the book. *Is this the "guiding light" that I'm supposed to follow?* It pointed toward an old cargo ship. At least, that's what she thought.

"Mr. Narrator," she whispered, "do I need to follow this light?"

"Yes, you do! Get on that ship! That's your one-way ticket!"

From the harbor, she saw a rope dangling off the edge of the ship and climbed up.

"I'm so glad that Jordan and I took that Spartan training course!"

The Narrator chuckled again. "Umm, the gangway is right over there."

Diana looked to her right and saw it. She ignored him and stuck with the challenge. As she reached the ship's deck, she rolled over and hit the floor with exhaustion. She covered her mouth as she felt her stomach turn.

The Narrator was amused. "Wow, you're one of those stubborn drunks."

Diana rolled her eyes before she burped. "Hell yeah."

When she got up, the guiding light had already disappeared. She didn't understand why. She thought that was her "one-way ticket" to escape the chapter. When she saw guards approaching the ship, she hid behind a couple of barrels and cloaked herself with the rough wool cloth that was draped over them. She couldn't risk being found. Crew members hoisted the sails and moved wooden crates as they complained about their journey to France. They all appeared to be in uniform—brown trousers with loose white tops.

She heard a loud horn, and realized that the ship was sailing away. Diana panicked and looked upward to get The Narrator's attention.

She whispered loudly for him to hear. "Hey! I thought I would be done here!"

The Narrator didn't respond.

"Hello?"

She felt the ship moving. She looked over the edge and noticed that they were getting farther and farther from the dock.

"Hey Narrator," she panicked. "There is no way that I'm going to France!"

Diana sat back against the barrels again and secured the wool around her. His lack of response made her angrier.

Seconds later, she was startled by the sounds of swords clashing and men yelling. Diana peeked over the barrels to see what the commotion was. Men in dark clothing swung from the ropes above her. Others fought and chased the crew members off the ship. Most of them voluntarily jumped overboard to swim back to shore. Diana debated whether she should do the same. She took a few steps back to reach the deck rail, but she felt a strong figure grab her from behind. His left arm hooked her around the waist, pressing her back against his chest. He used his other arm to hold his sword against the base of her throat. When he heard Diana make a frightful sound, he spun her around and ripped the wool from her body.

"A woman?" he murmured with shock.

Through the glow of torches, she could see his strong features. His long blond hair was tied back, showcasing his ocean blue eyes, chiseled jawline, and ashy stubble. Although his dark shirt was loose, she could still see the outline of his chest and his muscles. Some of his chest hairs curled above the collar, glinting gold in the torchlight. He placed his sword back in its sheath. He took a step closer and extended his hand toward her face. She flinched, but then realized he was only trying to pluck a rose thorn off her head. His voice and his wolfish smile made her quiver.

"Hold still."

It didn't take long for the fighting to come to an end. His men gathered behind Diana. "Cap'n found himself a floozy!" one of them yelled.

The others cheered and laughed while they fist-pumped the air. Diana's face was beet red as she turned around to face them. They looked like actual pirates—drunk and filthy. Believing that this situation wasn't real, she found the strength to boost her self-assurance. *This is a stupid dream, and I will be calling all the shots!*

"Excuse me!" she yelled at them.

They all stood in silence as she smirked. *Ha! Got their attention now.*

"First of all, I am a lady and you better damn well treat me as such!"

One man chuckled and mockingly bowed. "Our apologies, m'lady."

Diana pointed at him. "You, shut up."

But the men smirked and kept chattering to each other. It sounded like they were joking about her.

"Second of all," she said as she cleared her throat, "you are all filthy… what's the term? Ah yes, scallywags!"

There was a slight pause before they busted out in laughter.

"Diana!" The unexpected voice of The Narrator made her jump a little. "The word 'scallywag' won't be used for another 200 years."

"Oh, *now* you want to talk?" she grunted.

He chuckled. "I'm just trying to help."

"Well, you're doing such a wonderful job already! I don't speak pirate!"

She then noticed all of them staring at her in silence. "Oh wait, can they hear us talking?"

"Well, they can't hear *me* talking!"

One of the men approached her with a smile. "It seems that m'lady enjoys her own company more than she needs to."

He grabbed her arm and yanked her closer to him. The captain firmly gripped the other man's wrist until her arm was released. He then stepped in front of her, shielding her away from the others with the back of his arm.

"You will maintain your distance, bilge rat!"

The man chortled nervously and walked backward. When he made it to his group, another member knocked him out cold with a single punch. The majority again laughed until their captain approached. With one stern look, he made them stand straight in dead silence.

"Heed my warning. You will not touch her."

They all responded at once. "Aye, aye, Cap'n!"

The captain grabbed Diana's hand and pulled her closer to his side. "Now that we have taken what is rightfully ours, we shall journey westward! The wind is fair! Hoist the sail!"

"Aye, aye! Hoist the sail!"

She felt his gaze on her, but she looked everywhere but at him. He squeezed her hand a couple of times to get her attention. When she had the courage to look at his handsome face, he smiled. She couldn't resist and gave him a half-smile back. He took her hand and led her below deck to the captain's cabin, where he poured them each a cup of whisky.

He cleared his throat before speaking. "What's your name and what were you doing on my ship?"

Diana took a small sip and could taste its richness. "My name is Di... I mean Violet. Umm, was this really your ship to begin with?"

The captain laughed as he poured himself another cup. He tossed it back and smirked at her. She wasn't sure what was on his mind until he started to take his shirt off. She blushed and turned to face the door. Her heart raced as soon as she heard him unbuckle his belt and his trousers. *Is he for real?*

She could hear his footsteps approaching. *Oh my God! What's happening?* All she could think about was how to start up a quick conversation.

Her voice shook. "So . . . umm, Captain? You didn't tell me your name."

He wrapped his arms around her waist and pulled her close to his chest. She felt his heart beating against her back and looked down to see his hands loosening the front of her corset. She trembled as he gently kissed the nape of her neck. She could feel his warm breath in her hair as he whispered closely.

"Roger. You can call me Captain Roger."

He spun her around and pressed his lips firmly against hers. Diana's eyes widened before she jerked away from him. Still surrounded by his heat, she touched her shaking lips with her fingertips and could feel the warmth of his lingering kiss. She blushed and began to feel weak at the knees.

"Is this really happening?" she whispered to herself.

He drew her back toward him with his deep blue eyes and a smile.

She took a small step closer and pressed her hands to her beating heart, not sure how to proceed. He gently pulled her wrists toward the base of his neck and leaned in for a longer, more passionate kiss. Her eyes softened as she tilted her head beneath his. *This is really happening.*

His lips instantly sent stronger waves of pleasure along her nerves, arousing sensations that she thought she lacked. That rush of helplessness made her cling to him. He stopped their kiss for a moment to give her a reassuring, smoldering smile before bending down to wrap one arm under her knees. With the other hand, he supported her back. He leaned in for another kiss and carried her to his cot, where the passion set her aflame. His warm body was as hard as marble. The way he held her and caressed her beneath him put her in a euphoric daze. It almost felt too good to be true. Getting back at Tom with a sexy dream pirate seemed like the perfect revenge, which was such an unfortunate thought for that moment. Gone was the bone-melting heat and sensual daze; Diana was reduced to giggles and snorting.

The captain paused as he looked over her with surprised eyes and then chuckled with amusement. "Did m'lady just snort?"

Diana covered her mouth to hide her smile, but accidentally let out another snort. He grinned as he moved her hand away from her face and proceeded to kiss her below her ear. Her laughter was difficult to manage while she felt his soft, wet tongue tickling her skin. He let out a husky laugh before he pulled her waist closer to his. The firm grip of his hands made her gasp and hold her breath in. Between her thighs, she could feel his passion. She wrapped her legs around him and pulled him in for a deeper kiss. She wanted to enjoy the moment of whatever the heck this was, but then she heard The Narrator's sardonic voice.

"Oh Lady Violet, do you still think this is a dream?"

"Sure," Diana giggled.

"Interesting."

She smiled with her eyes closed. "Shh."

She laid in the captain's arms until he fell asleep. She wasn't able to rest as her mind replayed their time together. *This is the best sex dream that I ever had. It just felt so real, and the sad thing is, it felt even better than what I had with Tom.* The thought of Tom and what he did to her made her tear up again.

Suddenly, a small green flame flickered in front of the door. Diana lifted her head from the captain's bare chest and squinted her eyes to get a better view of it. Within seconds, the small flame ignited into a gigantic green orb and expanded into the shape of a round door. Charged electric currents spread out from its center, making sizzling sounds that grew louder until it sounded like a continuous electric thunder. Diana jumped out of bed and trembled with fear. She looked over the bed to find Captain Roger in a deep slumber. Her hands clutched his shoulders, and she shook him vigorously. The only response he gave her was a loud snore.

Her brows furrowed as she bit the side of her bottom lip. She glanced at the door again and sighed heavily. She braced herself with her eyes tightly shut before she faced it completely. She was stunned by its new appearance when she opened them. Its shape and electrifying vortex remained, but now instead of a circle, it looked more like an archway made of rectangular stones that shimmered green and silver. The intense sizzling sounds lessened into soft zaps and pops. *Is this the portal?*

The Narrator's voice erupted with excitement and made Diana jump. He spoke like a game show host. "You've completed Chapter 1. Congratulations!"

Diana tried to shield her nude body with her hands as she looked up. "What?"

"Just jump into the damn portal," The Narrator answered, annoyed, "and you'll wake up from your *dream.*"

She shrugged her shoulders and jumped in.

***

It was eight in the morning, and the power had come back on. The lights and the TV woke Diana from her slumber. She moaned as she felt an exploding pain shooting from behind her eyes. She rubbed them as she felt her temples throb. Her ears began to ache. The TV's volume was almost unbearable. Her hands searched blindly in front of her for the remote. A jingling sound forced her to pause and open an eye.

Bandit sat beside her, scratching his ear with his back paw. She looked around and found herself in Jordan's living room, as expected. Everything was intact. She looked down at herself and felt the softness of her flannels. A small chuckle escaped from her mouth. *For a second, I thought I was naked.* With a loud grunt, she managed to pull herself from the floor and turn to Bandit.

"You won't believe what kind of dream I just had."

He ran to the door and barked at her.

"Okay, I guess I better let you go potty."

She plugged in her phone and opened the back door to let him out. The yard was covered in snow. Its brightness nearly blinded her. Diana shook her head as she pressed her thumb into her forehead between her eyes. She felt her stomach heaving.

"You've got to be kidding me," she muttered. "Nope, not gonna deal with this."

Bandit finished his business quickly and ran back inside. Diana dropped a blanket over him and sat at the kitchen table, where she laid her head against its edge. Moments later, her phone rang. It was Jordan. Diana immediately answered—she needed to hear her friend's voice.

"Diana, are you there?"

Her voice shook. "Hi, Jordan. How is your trip?"

"Diana, what's wrong?"

She then sobbed. "T-Tom cheated."

"What?!"

She nodded as if her friend could see her. "He cheated on me with my coworker, and now I...I just don't know what to do."

"That son of a bitch!" Jordan raged. "I'm so sorry. I'll be on my way! Just sit tight, and we'll figure this whole thing out!"

She nodded again. "Okay."

Chapter 8

Diana made sure that the house was back in order and ready for Jordan's arrival. She packed up her things, even though she didn't know where she was going to live. She sat by the kitchen table and scrolled through her phone, searching for decent hotel rates. She didn't want to ask her parents if she could stay with them. The thought of living with them again immediately caused an unsettling pain in her stomach. *I can't. I promised myself I would never—*

Her phone chimed. Diana could feel her heart racing as her thumb pressed the icon. The automated voice on the other end instructed her to check her work email. Diana sighed heavily as she rolled her eyes. "Great. Can't wait."

A loud thump from the front porch startled her. Bandit ran to the front door as it was being pushed open. She rose from her seat when she saw Jordan walk in.

Jordan left her luggage at the door and waved a couple of takeout bags from their favorite restaurant. She met Diana's gaze with the corner of her mouth dipping down. She set the bags on the counter and ran to her for a long embrace. They spent the rest of the evening making cocktails, eating sushi, and discussing everything that had happened.

"I just don't know what to do, Jordan. How am I supposed to face Gwenyth at work tomorrow? Oh God, what will happen when I go back home to get my things?"

Jordan shook her head. "Do you even want to go to work tomorrow? I mean, Brenda is already giving you a hard time as it is."

Diana sighed. "I have to go back to work. She just sent me an email with a confirmed HR meeting. I need to be there at eight o'clock. I have a really bad feeling about this."

Jordan grabbed another piece of sushi and looked off to the side while she tapped her temple with the back of her chopsticks.

"I mean," Diana continued, "as long as I keep my head down, I should be okay, right?"

Jordan set her chopsticks down and started to crack her knuckles individually. "If you have to go to work, just ignore Gwenyth. I would also try reaching out to HR and advising them that Brenda is singling you out. You have those claim numbers, right? Use them to your advantage."

Diana nodded.

"As far as Tom goes, I get off work at two o'clock tomorrow," Jordan said. "I can go with you to pick up your things."

She teared up with relief. "Thank you. I just don't want to face him alone when I'm there."

"I get it. He's a gigantic asshole, but also a coward." Jordan cracked a small smile. "He won't say shit when I'm there, and even if he tries, he'll most definitely regret it."

Diana's phone chimed with another notification. Jordan glanced at Diana's screen, but snatched her phone before she could confirm the reservation. "And you're staying here with me. I will not have my best friend stay at a stupid hotel!"

Diana sniffled as more tears ran down her face. "How long can I stay? I don't want to impose."

Jordan smiled as she held her hand. "Stay here for as long as you need to. As a matter of fact, stay here for as long as you like."

"Thank you. Thank you for always being there. I definitely owe you."

"Of course! And you don't owe me anything, silly!"

The next morning, Diana drove to work with a clear conscience. Talking things through with Jordan helped her build a little more reassurance. She was finally going to take a stand against Brenda and show HR all her emails with the technical support tickets. She wasn't going to let her manager sabotage everything that she worked so hard for. She was also going to provide HR with all the claim numbers that she had to make corrections on from Gwenyth's poor handling. For months, Diana had sent formal complaints to Brenda about this issue, yet she had not taken any serious action. Diana smiled vengefully and gave herself a pep talk before she walked in.

"I can do this! Fuck Brenda and the horse she rode in on! And fuck that fake-ginger, plastic boob slut!"

Diana took a deep breath and marched down the hall with clenched fists. She could feel the blood pumping through her entire body. If someone wanted to fight her, she would be ready for it. As soon as she approached her station, she noticed her cubicle was completely empty. All of her personal items were gone. Brenda walked out of her office with two security guards. One guard held a small box and the other, a giant man, stood there with his arms crossed. He smirked as if he knew pain was coming to someone that was not him.

Gwenyth and her friends stood nearby for the newest episode of *Diana's Embarrassing Life*. They all giggled as Brenda and the guards walked Diana toward the exit. Apparently, talking to HR was out of the question. Brenda told her she had been terminated and that it was pointless to argue against it. Brenda took the box from the security guard and shoved it at Diana, snatched her ID card off her neck, and stood there as the security guards escorted her out of the building. They walked her to her car and advised her that she needed to leave the premises immediately.

Diana didn't know how to react. She was silent on her way to Jordan's. She didn't remember arriving at her house or even getting out and locking the car. She sat on the couch, staring blankly at the ceiling. The second she felt Bandit sit beside her feet, she jerked and muttered to herself.

"Fuck my life. How could this happen? It's like one thing after another. It's like *The NeverEnding Story* with me. Like, why?"

Without much thought, she grabbed one of the teal throw pillows beside her, and violently pressed it against her face. She let out a long, muffled shriek before she picked up her phone to text Jordan.

Diana: *Guess who got fired.*

Diana fanned her face with her hand as burning tears dripped down her cheeks. Jordan's response was what she needed.

Jordan: *I'm here for you.*

As she waited for Jordan's return, she texted Tom that she was going to be at the apartment around two o'clock to get her things, but he didn't respond.

As soon as Jordan made it home, they loaded her Range Rover with empty boxes and tote bags.

"You know, this could easily be a wrongful termination lawsuit," Jordan told her.

"Ugh, please no. I don't want to waste any more of my life on a job that I've always hated. Plus, how am I going to afford to sue anyone without a job?"

"Okay, I get that. Just don't let this get you down," Jordan encouraged. "I'll help you find a better job, and you know you don't have to worry about paying rent. You're doing your part by keeping Bandit company."

"Are you sure? You've done so much for me."

Jordan smiled. "Things will turn up. You just need to have a little faith and patience."

Diana sighed. "I know. Thank you for helping me get through all this crap."

"Absolutely. I know you would do the same thing for me if I was in this situation," Jordan said. "Besides, everyone goes through these ridiculous trials. You just had most of them hit you at once. Hopefully, you'll be good for the rest of your life."

They both burst into laughter.

"I don't know. Somehow, I feel like things might get worse."

Jordan glanced at her with a smirk. "Okay, you're on. I bet you a quarter."

"Why only a quarter?"

Jordan snorted and bit her tongue.

"Is this because I'm poor and my life is a shit show?"

They both laughed again. Maybe things weren't as bad as Diana felt.

Before walking into Diana's apartment, Jordan grabbed her hand. "I'm here for you every step of the way. There's nothing to worry about with Tom. It's all bigger and better from here. This new chapter is going to be the best yet!"

The chapter reference threw Diana for a loop as she remembered her time with Captain Roger. She shook the memory off and opened the front door.

"What the hell is that smell?" Jordan asked, covering her nose.

"That's her perfume. She wears that a lot at work."

"Gross. Where should we start packing?"

Diana pointed to her bedroom. "All my clothes should be in there."

As they walked down the hall, Diana noticed that Gwenyth had already started settling in. Their bathroom was full of unfamiliar hair products and makeup. Her toothbrush was already next to Tom's. Diana and Jordan rolled their eyes at each other as they scoped the place out.

"Well, I guess Tom and Slutty McSlutters didn't waste any time," Jordan said.

As Diana opened the bedroom door, she was taken aback. It had been redesigned with fancier floral bedding, new lamps, and a new couple's picture on their dresser. It took her a second to realize that the picture was taken during the spring. The trees were green and full of life, and they were in formal attire. Gwenyth was in a red dress while Tom was in a navy fitted suit. From the scenery, she saw large, white cloth tables behind them with candlelight centerpieces on them. *Could that have been someone's wedding?* Diana sighed as she turned away. *They were together longer than I thought. Oh man . . . that homewrecker said a year when we talked at the office!*

The moment she opened her closet door, she panicked. All of her clothes and shoes were gone. She ran to her their dresser and found her side was replaced with Gwenyth's things.

"Jordan!" she yelled. "I can't find my things." They searched everywhere and couldn't find her clothes, her books, or even her personal hygiene products. It was as if she had never existed.

Diana texted Tom again, demanding to where her belongings were. Jordan took Diana's phone and called Tom, but the scumbag did not answer. After a couple minutes passed, they finally received a text from him.

> **Tom:** *You said you would be back in a couple of days to pick up your shit. I waited patiently til nine this morning. If you have any luck, you'll be able to find your clothes at the Goodwill down the street.*

Jordan's jaw dropped. "You mean to tell me that he waited exactly two days on the dot? Did you know about this time limit?"

Diana managed to laugh while tears ran down her face. "Seems like things did get worse. I guess you owe me that quarter now."

Her friend was visibly livid. "That fucking asshole! He's gonna regret this!"

Diana sobbed as she was pulled in for a long hug. She wanted revenge, but kept telling herself that Tom was not worth the trouble. She wanted to wreck the entire place and cut out the crotch of every pair of his pants, but she knew better. She did not want to be as petty as him, and she most definitely didn't want to play his sick little games anymore. The best thing for her to do was to move on with her life. When she was ready to leave, she placed her key on the kitchen counter and shut the door behind them.

Chapter 9

On the drive home, they decided that they needed an ultimate girl's night with takeout, wine, and chick flicks in their pajamas. Jordan set up the spare bedroom with fresh sheets and extra pillows. Diana ordered food and skimmed through movie selections. After the details were confirmed, she moved to the couch and poured each of them a glass of merlot.

"So, champ, how are you holding up?"

Diana sipped her wine. "I'll be okay. I just hope I get back on my feet soon is all."

Jordan patted her shoulder. "You will *and* you will find someone who will cherish you and treat you like the queen that you are!"

Diana nodded as they clinked their glasses.

"Also, don't worry about clothes," Jordan continued. "We're about the same size anyway. You can borrow mine, especially for interviews!"

"You're seriously the best friend anyone could ask for."

"I know," Jordan laughed. "You got lucky."

They ended up watching *Working Girl,* one of their favorites. In it, a woman risks her job and relationships all so that she can just survive—maybe some of her luck and determination would rub off on Diana. Bandit snuggled in between them until it was time for bed.

Diana glanced at her new bedroom as she settled under the covers. She could smell the clean sheets, and she had plenty of pillows to snuggle with. Jordan had done everything to make this feel like her new home. She didn't feel like she had to be on guard every second like she had been with Tom. Still, the room felt empty. Everything that she owned was folded and stacked in a tiny pile on the carpet beside her.

"A new chapter, a new beginning," she whispered to herself. She was exhausted, but she also felt oddly calm. Maybe she was starting to feel numb after everything that happened. *Could the worst be really over though? Tomorrow has to be a better day. There's no choice but to move forward, right?*

The next morning, Bandit woke them up around six. Diana made coffee while Jordan did a quick workout in her basement. Normally, Diana would take every opportunity to share a workout with Jordan, but today she was on a mission to get her life back on track. After they made breakfast, Diana borrowed Jordan's laptop to start job hunting.

"I'll check for open clerical positions at the firm, too," Jordan offered. "It might not pay much, but at least it's something."

"Any job I can get immediately is good enough for me. I mean, I just came from *shark insurance.*"

Jordan tried not to laugh as she headed out the door for work.

Diana spent another three hours researching before taking a little break. She grabbed her phone to check for any missed calls or texts, but eventually got suckered into spying on Tom through his social media profile. On the very day she caught him cheating, he had updated his relationship status and profile picture. It was the same photo she spotted on their dresser. Of course, Tom waited for the right opportunity to post it.

"Well, isn't this the picture-perfect couple?" she muttered as she rolled her eyes.

She couldn't resist the urge to read everyone's comments and see what their "mutual friends" had to say. They had liked her . . . or so she thought. Apparently, he had been complaining about Diana behind her back for a while. They all approved of his new girlfriend, and some had already commented that he "upgraded." She chucked her phone across the room and walked out the French doors into the backyard. It wasn't as cold as it was a couple days ago. Most of the snow had already melted, revealing Jordan's lawn and her empty fire pit. A small line of pots that once held vibrant chrysanthemums separated the grass from the stamped patio flooring. Bandit accompanied her to the mosaic table that sat across from Jordan's grilling station, but there was nothing he could do to help her escape her negative thoughts. *It's no wonder. I'm not sexy. I'm not pretty. I'm just a low-life loser.*

After wallowing in self-pity, she took a shower and browsed Jordan's closet. "Of course, she mostly has high-waisted leggings and crop tops!" Diana either had to get out of her comfort zone and deal with it or she had to spend the little money she had saved on newer clothes. She clenched her jaw and secured the bath towel around her.

"Decisions, decisions," she muttered.

She groaned with a sudden pain that doubled her over. "What the hell?"

She pressed her arm against her abdomen. *I've felt this before, but...*

When she stepped out of the closet, she heard powerful winds approaching. The first thing that came to mind was another storm, but neither of the trees outside the bedroom window were moving. Bandit yelped and then took refuge under Jordan's bed. Wincing in pain, Diana clutched onto her towel and knelt down next to the bed to get him, but he recoiled from her reach.

"Bandit, what's wrong?"

The bedroom door swung open as a massive cyclone burst through. She screamed, but the wind was so ferocious that she felt like her screams were snatched from her throat. All she heard was the wind. It howled at her as its strong pressure lifted her up off the carpet. Diana reached her hands out to grab onto something, anything. Before she knew it, the winds sent her spinning around the room. She gave up on grabbing hold of something and instead tried desperately to keep her towel around her. It ripped out from under her hands, and she could only watch it playfully fly just out of her reach every time she went to snatch it.

A multitude of thoughts rushed through her head at once. She imagined that she was either possessed by a demon or that Jordan's house was majorly haunted. The last thing she saw was that creepy old book sitting on the floor. The wind held her in a hover over it for a moment until the book opened on its own. A bright green neon light beamed from it and shone through her to the ceiling. The pages rapidly turned, then stopped when it reached the second chapter. As the surrounding winds spun faster, she felt her body being pulled down. It was at that moment—and she had no idea why it took her this long—that she realized she was being sucked into the book. Her last words echoed with panic.

"Holy shiiit!"

BAM! Diana clenched her jaw as she rubbed her backside.

"Ow!" As soon as she opened her eyes, she took notice of the floor. "Marble flooring? Where am I now?"

She was wearing clothes, but didn't know how she got into them. She was dressed in a long pink silk gown with golden embellishments and beading that jingled with every movement she made.

Her arms were wrapped with gold jewelry with pink stones from her elbows to her wrists. Her hair was darker and longer, but it was perfectly styled in waves. She felt a weighted headpiece resting on her temples. It was trailed by more beading with a sheer veil that caped around her shoulders and back. As she picked herself off the floor, she noticed her flat, pointy shoes. They were also covered with gold embellishments and shimmering precious stones.

Diana looked at her surroundings. The room was bright, with stone bricks and large unglazed windows. The sunlight entered the room and made the stone floor and walls glisten. A gentle wind made the white draperies flutter calmly into the room. Across from her, two solid doors bore golden floral designs.

She was curious what was behind them, but the beautiful songs of birds made her peek outside first. Diana was amazed at what she saw. Tall, white-stoned towers topped with golden domes surrounded her. Every corner had an exotic flower garden, which explained why the air smelled so fresh. It was like she was in an ancient, enchanted palace.

"Am I in Heaven?" she whispered to herself. "How did I die?"

A familiar voice playfully laughed at her. "You're not dead, silly."

She jumped. "Who's there?"

The laughter echoed around the room. "Oh, so you don't remember?"

She spun around a few times, but couldn't see anyone. "Why can't I see you?"

Damn, I love his voice. She blushed as she used her hand to cover her smile.

"I knew it," the voice said playfully.

Her face turned white. "Can you read my mind? Are you my conscience?"

He laughed even harder. "I thought that you were a fun drunk, but this takes the cake! I'm your narrator. You used your only wish for me to sound like this."

Diana took a step back and remembered her so-called "dream" with Captain Roger.

The Narrator noticed the horror of reality spreading across her face. "And . . . welcome back," he teased.

"So, I-I wasn't dreaming?" she stuttered.

"Nope."

"Wait! That means that you saw me?"

"What?"

"You saw me with the captain!"

"Oh . . . yeah," he replied. "Amazing performance, by the way."

Diana's face turned red as she cringed with disgust. "You pervert! Oh, I'm so grossed out right now!"

The Narrator sighed. "Well, I suppose you'll get used to it. You'll forget that I'm even around most of the time."

"What do you mean by that? How did this happen? Also, what's with that creepy book? It opened by itself!"

"Well, you see," he continued, "I only exist to guide you through each chapter. That 'creepy book' was gifted to you by someone with incredible powers and now you must read it from start to finish. You're only given a certain amount of time off from it. You need to read through every chapter willingly or it will suck you in. It says so in the rules."

"What rules?" Diana asked sternly.

"Oh my God, you seriously don't remember anything!" he shouted. "Rule 1: Finish every chapter when expected. This is important for you to remember! Rule 2: Follow the guiding lights. Rule 3: You are permitted bookmarks. Rule 4: You have one emergency escape to exit. Rule 5 no longer applies to you because you're a dumbass. And last, but not least, Rule 6: Enjoy the pleasures that await you."

Diana stood in silence for a moment. "So let me get this straight," she said with an attitude. "I've been cursed to read this whole damn book, and I'm chained to it until I finish it?"

"I wouldn't call it a curse, but basically."

She counted on her fingers. "The guiding lights are there to help me finish and leave every chapter."

"Uh-huh."

"I also have to listen to you . . . and deal with the fact that you'll be watching me."

"Ding, ding, ding!" The Narrator responded enthusiastically. "We have a winner!"

She shut her eyes tightly and then pursed her lips before speaking further. "Enjoy the pleasures that await me? You mean—"

The Narrator chuckled. "Do you need me to elaborate on that?"

Diana shook her head. "I got the gist of it, but what happens if I don't want to?"

"Then you'll be stuck and you will not be able to leave the chapters," he stated plainly. "I highly doubt that you'll want to refuse, though."

Diana opened her eyes. "You don't know me, and I'm not a slave!"

"Nobody is holding a gun to your head."

"Ha!" she yelled. "You might as well be! I didn't ask for this curse! Getting 'The D' in every chapter from complete strangers? Gross!"

"It's a gift," he grunted. "You will see!"

Diana remembered what the store owner said: *Do you not know how to say thank you when receiving a gift?*

She also remembered how she tried to refuse the book, but felt compelled to take it. *Ugh, what the hell have I gotten myself into now? I should have run away when I had the chance!* She straightened herself before asking him another question.

"Who is this witch, by the way?"

He sighed again. "I'm not at liberty to say. Her powers are vast. Even if I tried, my words would be muted."

"That's a bunch of bull." She crossed her arms and grunted with frustration. "You can't even give me a clue?"

"Nope."

"Fine. What about the bookmarks? The stupid book didn't come with them."

"They're not physical bookmarks, Diana. You just yell the word, 'bookmark' and it will pause everything. They will definitely come in handy when you need time to think, but just know your pause time is very limited."

Diana rolled her eyes and exhaled deeply. "Crap . . . okay. Well, I need to get out of here. I didn't get the chance to read this chapter because I was sucked in *against my will!*"

The Narrator laughed. "Don't make this into a bigger deal than it really is."

Her arms remained crossed as she looked up with disgust. "So, who do I have to fuck to get out of here?"

She heard another man's voice coming from behind the doors. "Oh, Ariana?"

Diana jumped from where she stood. She whispered loudly to The Narrator. "Am I this Ariana character?"

"Yes, you're a palace concubine! Now get going!"

"What! A concubine?" she whispered more aggressively. "You must be joking!"

The man's voice grew more demanding. "Ariana! Where is that girl? Guards, bring her to me now! I've been waiting long enough!"

Diana flinched as she heard the doors open. She took notice of how the light from the other side expanded down the marble flooring.

Her golden shoes shimmered. She looked up at the two guards who appeared before her. They both had loose, dark attire; long, dark beards bejeweled with gold beading; and black turbans. One guard crossed his arms in front of her and gave her a serious look. The other smiled at her and gripped the handle of his shamshir sword, which was tied to his banded waist. The moment she gazed at them reminded her of her favorite childhood movie. What was next? A genie and a magic carpet? Suddenly, the three of them heard the man's voice grow impatient from the other side.

"Well?" he demanded.

The guards motioned for her to enter the room. Diana took a deep breath and dramatically waltzed in. She even threw in a couple of theatrical spins.

The Narrator scoffed at her. "You must be joking."

Diana, of course, ignored him and started humming *A Whole New World*. She wanted to at least have some enjoyment with her misery.

The guard who had previously smiled at her couldn't hold back his laughter. He had never seen such obnoxious behavior, especially from a concubine. The other guard thumped him with the side of his fist and shut the doors behind them. "Quiet, you fool!" She heard him yell at his companion. "You will be lucky if the prince did not hear you!"

"A prince?" Diana whispered to herself. "This might actually be good."

She was amazed as she looked around the prince's room. Everything was covered in gold— golden furniture, golden draperies, golden rugs, and golden trinkets. She heard the man's voice from the canopy bed in the back of the room.

"Stop," he demanded.

Diana froze and turned to face him, but she still couldn't see who was behind the silk curtains.

She did see a couple of fan-bearers on each side of his bed. They fanned him with large peacock feathers attached to long golden rods. The women were dressed similarly to her, but they wore turquoise and had half of their faces covered with veils. As soon as he commanded them to leave, the women dropped their fans and took off. Diana heard the bed sheets ruffle as he grunted his way out.

She closed her eyes and began to tremble. *I seriously hope he's not hideous.* She imagined The Narrator secretly laughing somewhere behind the scenes. Who wouldn't, though? Her life was a joke at this point. She gulped as she heard his footsteps approach her. Her eyes flew open when she felt his hand lightly grasp her chin.

She was stunned by how gorgeous this man was. He was tall and muscular with olive skin. His dark beard was short and neatly groomed. Although he wasn't fully dressed, it was obvious that he was royalty. He wore a sheer tunic that revealed his bare chest and abs. It was long enough to cover his body, but it was only loosely tied together. Her fingertips tingled and jerked just as he lifted her head to meet his gaze. He had striking dark eyes. She didn't know whether to fear him or be consumed by him.

His whisper was deep and full of lust. "What kept you, my sweet? I've been longing, waiting, aching, for you."

Diana felt a shiver down her spine and didn't know how to respond. She spoke softly. "I'm . . . sorry?"

He lightly pressed his forehead against hers and leaned in for a kiss. She gasped with surprise. *Wow, getting right to it.*

When their lips almost met, he pulled himself away from her and smirked. It seemed that he was playing a game that he only knew the rules to. *Is he teasing?* She didn't know what to make of this guy. From his pocket, he pulled out a juicy plum and took a bite.

"Would you like one?" he asked.

Diana shyly nodded.

"That's too bad." He grinned and took another bite.

He carelessly tossed the fruit over his shoulder and stripped off his clothes. "Gaze upon my perfection," he demanded with arrogance.

Her attraction dissipated as Diana realized this guy was a spoiled brat with no game. *That was a jerk move—offering me food and then throwing it away.* Forgetting where she was, she rolled her eyes and shook her head with disappointment. He took notice of her expression and stormed over. He clutched onto a strand of her hair, pulling enough to get her attention.

"Do you know what I'm capable of? I am Jafeer, the most powerful—"

Her insane laughter cut him off. "Jafeer? More like Jafar!"

She couldn't hold it in anymore and started laughing. And then kept laughing. *I mean really? Who does this guy think he is?* She found herself in a loop of trying to stifle her laughter, only to be drawn back in by his incredulous expression. Despite her efforts to contain it, the sight of his disbelieving face ignited her laughter, creating a cycle that seemed impossible to break. It probably wasn't the smartest decision to make fun of him to his face. And although he was more handsome than the most conniving villain of all time, the name similarity was so befitting for his character. It was obvious that Jafeer didn't like feeling excluded or humiliated. His dark eyes flooded with wrath. He took immediate action to correct her behavior, viciously grasping a huge chunk of her hair. He pulled it with enough force to make her wince.

"Who is this Jafar?" he grunted with anger.

Diana felt his knuckles tighten and she reached her hand behind her head to try to stop him from grasping her hair even tighter. The skin behind her ear throbbed in pain as he pulled more. It was shocking that she was able to feel pain. *Isn't this just a story that I have to play a part of? Could I seriously get hurt? Could I die in this book?* She saw the anger and jealousy in this man's eyes. She had to wise up and say something—quickly.

Her voice shook. "Oh! He's . . . nobody important, my love."

He seemed pleased with her sudden subservience. A drastic change came over his face—his eyes no longer narrowed with anger and Diana's eyes were drawn to his lips that were now in a relaxed smile. His grip on her hair didn't immediately loosen. Instead, it felt as though his fingers were massaging her tingling scalp. And that tingle shot like lightening straight to the center of her, causing her to gasp. When he fully loosened his grip, he cupped her cheek as if she was something precious—as if he hadn't just been about to rip a huge clump of hair out of her head and leave her partially bald.

"That's what I thought," he whispered. "Nobody."

He grabbed both of her arms and pulled her in for a passionate kiss. Diana instinctively pushed him off and shrieked. The man did have strong lips, though, and she felt weak at the knees. The passion was there, but also fear. She took a few steps back, only to find out that he was ready to chase after her.

"Bookmark!" Everything froze instantly. She saw Jafeer's tantalizing smile. His back was slightly curled as he prepared to pounce on her. She called out to The Narrator in panic.

"Yoo-hoo! Over here! I want out!"

He chuckled. "Are you seriously giving up that easily?"

"He's such a jerk," she retorted as she stomped her foot.

"Let's cut the crap. You have the hots for this guy. Just have fun and don't overthink it," he urged.

"He hurt me! I didn't know that I could feel pain in this book! Like, can I be killed?"

The Narrator laughed. "Well, nobody has died *yet*."

Her anxiety grew as he continued.

"If you were smart, you would be seeking pleasure instead."

She sighed deeply and looked at Jafeer's face once more. She gave herself a short pep talk. "Okay, I can do this. I can do this. I can—"

"I hate to interrupt," The Narrator shouted, "but your break is coming to an end in three, two, one!"

The chapter resumed. Diana made the decision to just go with it. What other choice did she have? Jafeer approached her.

"Now, where were we? Ah, yes!"

She shrieked again as he swept her off her feet. She was surprised by how quickly he could arouse her by simply holding her with his strong arms. She could feel the blood rushing to her cheeks. *Was that all it took?* When he took notice of her body trembling beneath his grasp, he maliciously laughed and trotted over to his bed. She nervously laughed with him before he threw her on his mattress, and with no time to waste, he flung himself on top of her.

Being kissed and caressed made her want more, but the fear of displeasing him was in the back of her mind. She wanted to forget his flaws and his aggression, but didn't really know what to expect. She didn't have much experience; he only knew what Tom liked, and she was too drunk to even remember whether Captain Roger was pleased. Tom's words echoed in her head: *"One of the lousiest lays of my life."*

She needed to play the role of concubine perfectly, but she didn't know how. And was she really going to enjoy this?

Her concerned expression was easy to read, but Jafeer didn't care enough to ask what ailed her. He lifted her to her knees and wrapped his arms around her waist. His firm body pressed against hers. She came around to the thought of enjoying him. *Maybe The Narrator was right. He's gorgeous, and how many opportunities like this will I get?* His scent of rose and musk intoxicated her. When Diana began untying her gown, Jafeer seized her hand with his own. She was stunned. *What now?*

He smirked as he whispered in her ear. "My pleasure always comes first, my love."

Diana figured out what he meant and hoped that she was wrong. *Great.* The very thought of satisfying him annoyed her. She didn't want to waste another bookmark, but she wanted to know what the exact purpose of the book was if she wasn't going to "enjoy the pleasures that awaited her." She thought this book was for her enjoyment only.

Jafeer leaned over the edge of the bed and plucked a large peacock feather from one of the rods the fanners had left. He placed it in her hand and smirked. Seconds later, Diana found herself with eyes wide and mouth agape. Jafeer turned his back to her and moved to all fours.

"Umm . . ."

"You know what to do," Jafeer grunted, "so do it."

He arched his back and leaned his backside toward her. Diana rolled her eyes and silently yelled at the ceiling with a clenched fist. "What the fuck?"

The Narrator just laughed.

She took a deep breath to ease her frustration, but made sure that Jafeer didn't hear her. She had to appease his weird demands to get out of this silly chapter. As soon as she began tickling his ass, Jafeer got up to face her and slammed her flat on her back. She was scared beyond belief. *Oh crap, I knew that I wasn't supposed to tickle him there!*

Jafeer snatched the feather from her hand and then tightly grabbed onto her right ankle. Her instincts told her to run, but his grip was so intense! There was no escape. He had her right where he wanted. Diana shut her eyes tightly and feared the unknown. His malicious laugh grew louder as she screamed with panic, but it all came to an end when she felt him place the feather in between her toes. Her shocking reaction made him laugh even harder, but at least he was not persistent with violence. He shook his head and then went back to his favorite position.

"Do it," he commanded.

Diana gulped and started moving her foot up and down, using the feather as a toy. From that moment, it was evident that Jafeer loved his ass being tickled by her feet. Spelling out "sick creep" with her foot was entertaining enough, as he had no clue. His ugly and obnoxious grunts, however, were a bit much for her to handle. Her leg was hurting with the effort of keeping it in the necessary position. Trying to get through it, she leaned all the way back and placed her hand behind her knee so it could further support her calf as she trailed the feather across his ass. The sounds he was making weirded her out to the point where she wanted to stop, but he wouldn't allow it. *I just want to kick him.*

She didn't have much time to think. As she worked her foot, she looked around the room for any additional help. A golden vase next to his bed caught her eye. She quickly grabbed it and smashed it over his head. He rolled off the bed, moaning.

Diana sprinted to the doors, screaming. "Shit, fuck! Shit, fuck! Shit, shit, shit, fuck!"

The Narrator laughed uncontrollably. "You are absolutely my favorite host, but seriously? What is your next move?"

She yanked one of the doors open. "I need to get out of here!"

The two guards were already waiting for her with their swords drawn. "Bring that girl to me, now!" Jafeer commanded.

Diana gulped as they approached her. She wasn't sure how intelligent these men were, so she pointed to the ceiling and screamed. "What's that over there?"

One guard looked up. The other one bopped him on the head again.

She couldn't sneak her way out this time, but then she remembered what The Narrator advised about using an emergency escape. "Narrator!" she yelled, "I want to use my emergency escape exit!"

The guards whispered amongst themselves. "Who is she talking to?"

"I'm not sure."

"Are you sure?" The Narrator responded. "You might regret it."

Jafeer's voice grew with anger. "I will kill that whore!"

The guards smiled at her and paced themselves. She didn't want to give it a second thought.

"I'm positive! Get me the hell out of here!" she screamed.

"Escape granted!" he shouted back.

Within the blink of an eye, everything froze again. Only this time, a huge green light blasted from everywhere, piercing through the walls and ceiling. Diana shielded her eyes from its intensity. The scenery faded and crumbled. Her vision blurred as she heard the sound of its power softening. Within seconds, it finally went silent. She could feel Jordan's carpet beneath her bare feet. When she opened her eyes, she found herself in her own room, naked. The book laid flat beside her. Her towel fell from the ceiling and landed on her head. She was back in her world.

Chapter 10

It didn't take Diana long to throw on some clothes and rush to her car. Returning the damn book seemed like the best solution. Even though it had clasps, she wrapped duct tape around it. She couldn't take any chances. She wanted to get her life back on track, not make it more complicated.

She had never believed in witchcraft until this book came along. The roads were still a bit slippery, and she had to calm herself before having another meltdown. "How could this happen? Like why? This is some crap that only happens in books and movies. Of course! It's because it's *me*! Fuck... my life *is* like *The NeverEnding Story*. More like *The NeverEnding Fucking Story*!"

When she pulled into the bookstore's parking lot, her heart stopped. A huge red sign on the door of the building read *Condemned*. She grabbed the book and ran to the door. Diana yanked onto the handle and shook it, but it wouldn't budge. She peeked through the broken glass and saw the entire store was a mess.

The ceiling had collapsed, causing a major flood inside. No wonder the sign stated it was "unfit for human occupancy." Diana howled with dismay and fell to her knees.

"What am I supposed to do?" Suddenly, an epiphany. "I know what to do with you!"

Back at the house, Diana set the book on Jordan's kettle grill and drenched it with lighter fluid. She lit a match and smiled maliciously. "There's nothing in your 'rules' that says I can't."

She apprehensively flicked it into the grill and slammed the lid shut. She took a few steps back. "This has to work."

When she saw the flames and black smoke rise, she felt immediate relief. "Hallelujah! Burn in—"

A loud growling made her pause. The grill shook vigorously, as if it contained some angry creature. Popping the lid clean off, the book rose from the grate and floated into the air. Diana screeched as she witnessed it changing in front of her. The duct tape burned off, and the book glowed red as the center of its front cover caved in. Within seconds, it formed sharp teeth and black beady eyes. It flew in front of her face, nearly biting the tip of her nose.

Usually in nature, when danger arises, a person or animal reacts with a fight or flight response. Well, in Diana's case, she just stood there like a damn ostrich. The book set her straight with its incessant snarls and barks. All she could do was close her eyes, shake uncontrollably, and take it until she collapsed. After making its point, the book changed back to its original form and fell flat next to her. Hot sweat rolled down her back. Her bottom lip trembled with fear. She apologized to the book and ran to the bathroom to take the biggest dump of her life.

After calming herself for a couple hours, she was strong enough to retrieve the book from the yard. She went into her bedroom and set it nicely on her pillow. Destroying the book was out of the question, and returning it seemed impossible. "Ugh, why did I go in that damn store? Why didn't I ask that lady's name? Well . . . more like that witch!"

Diana opened Jordan's laptop to see whether A BookStore had a website or any contact information. The address wasn't even listed online. Diana sat on the edge of the bed with her hands pressed over her face. She tried to come up with other ways of avoiding the book, but it seemed that the only way out was to finish reading it.

"Fine," she glared at the book with fear and frustration. "You win."

Exhaustion claimed most of the day. Diana, still traumatized, needed to focus on something else. At least she wasn't thinking about Tom. Luckily, Bandit never left her side. The puppy comforted her until she heard Beethoven's haunting symphony. She jolted from her spot and snatched her phone from the kitchen counter. She could feel her stomach turning. Once again, she immediately ended the call, but sent her mother a text.

> **Diana:** Mom, I seriously can't talk right now.

To maintain her sanity, she turned to cooking. She knew how much Jordan loved spicy food, so she made her famous chicken chili casserole. As she placed it into the oven, her phone chimed with an email notification. She perked up, hoping for good news. It was an interview request from a local book editing firm, The Welcome Reader, for an assistant position. She read through the job description, but she did not remember applying. She felt a bit discouraged, since she did not have the years of experience they sought. Still, intuition persuaded her to follow through. She crossed her fingers, then clicked the Accept button to schedule a time.

Jordan made it home from work about an hour later, just as Diana pulled the dish out of the oven. The wonderful aroma was irresistible. They grabbed their plates and rushed to the kitchen table. As Jordan poured wine into their glasses, they spoke at the same time.

"I have great news!" they shouted.

"Jinx!" they said in unison again.

"Buttercup!" they shouted as they cackled.

"Okay, okay." Jordan continued laughing. "Tell me your news first, and then I'll tell you mine."

"I got an interview."

Jordan clapped and cheered. "Woo!"

"Well, don't get too excited yet," Diana said before taking a small sip.

Jordan raised a brow. "What do you mean? Is it something boring?"

"Oh, I'm very interested. It's for an editor's assistant position for The Welcome Reader."

"Oh my *God*!"

Diana nodded and smiled. "Yep!"

"Wait, how could I not be excited for you? This is an amazing opportunity."

"I don't meet their criteria. I lack the experience. All I have are my good grades and—"

"And that two-year internship that you said was a 'waste of your time?'" Jordan scoffed playfully. "Girl, you got this in the bag! You just need to be confident!"

Diana nodded with folded lips. "I just don't know how they found me, though. I don't even remember applying."

Jordan pondered a bit. "Maybe it was an old application submission that they kept on file? Oh, wait a minute! Didn't you apply a year ago?"

Her eyes turned to the ceiling as she took a moment to think. "You know what . . . you might be right."

Jordan smiled and clinked her glass against Diana's. "You got this, sis. Cheers."

After another sip, Diana stared at Jordan. "Your turn."

"My turn, eh?" Jordan gulped, regretting her announcement. "Umm . . . not sure if I want to tell you just yet."

"What?!" Diana jumped out of her seat. "Not fair! You spill whatever secret you have or I'm gonna—"

"Okay, okay! I sort have been . . . seeing someone."

"Oh my God! This is so great!" Diana slid forward in her seat. "So, you have a boyfriend now?"

She shut her eyes as she let out a long sigh. "Ugh, I hate that word. Technically, yes. I do."

Diana bounced in her chair. "This is the best news!"

Jordan had an issue with saying the word boyfriend because she never had much luck finding Mr. Right. In fact, Jordan never mentioned even having an ex. She was extremely picky with men. Many had argued that her friend had unrealistic standards, saying chivalry was dead for the modern-day man. Tom called her a frigid lesbian behind her back and often claimed she had a secret crush on Diana. Deep down, Diana knew he was wrong. If anything, she had a small—but innocent—crush on Jordan. She was always envious of her friend and wished she could live her life.

"So," Diana continued, "who is he and what does he do?"

Jordan took a gulp of her wine. "Well, umm . . . it's classified."

"What?"

"I cannot tell you who it is."

Her cautious tone left Diana bewildered, for a moment.

"Jordan . . . is it an athlete that you're in contract with?"

She pursed her lips and nodded shamefully.

Diana gasped. "Oh my *God*! Can you at least give me a clue?"

"One clue and that's it," Jordan said sternly.

"Well, make it a good one at least," Diana bit her thumb.

"Soccer."

She banged the side of her fist against the table. "You work with seven teams!"

Jordan smirked. "That's all I can tell you for now."

"How long have you been with this guy? Couldn't have been that long, right?"

Jordan took another gulp. "We've known each other for a while, but now things are getting more serious. . . That's all the information you're gonna get, missy!"

Diana's jaw dropped. "Thank God for Google. I'm gonna do some research!"

Jordan shook her head and laughed, "You better not!"

Diana ferreted out a few more details, such as his height and eye color, but it was not enough to confirm who he was. As much as Jordan wanted to tell her friend everything, she had to maintain her composure. Diana could tell from the way Jordan pulled her mouth sideways and flattened her brows that there was more to discuss, but she chose not to probe any further.

Another email from The Welcome Reader confirmed her interview: Nine-thirty the day after tomorrow. The fear was already settling in, but Jordan was an excellent hype woman.

"I know you're already doubting yourself, but we are *not* doing that!" Jordan assured her. "Tomorrow, let's pick out an outfit that says, 'I mean business,' and then we can practice some interview questions."

"You are my hero!" Diana beamed. "But for now, let's watch some more trashy reality TV."

Diana dreaded heading back to her room. The thought of opening the door made her shudder since the grilling incident. She thought that nearly crapping her pants was a well-deserved punishment, but she couldn't help but wonder if the book held some resentment toward her. Did it have the ability to conspire against her, or worse—attack her in her sleep? She quietly cracked open her door, allowing a sliver of light to enter before her. She found the book where she left it—resting on her pillow. She held a deep breath in as she felt the hot sweat trickle down her back again. *Okay, I know what I need to do.*

She didn't want to leave the book just lying around the house, especially for Jordan to find. She ran inside her bedroom, placed it under her bed, and then ran out the door. Sleeping on the couch with the TV on seemed ideal, at least for the night.

Chapter 11

The next morning, they rummaged through Jordan's wardrobe and found the perfect outfit for Diana's interview. She was amazed by how flawless she looked in Jordan's slim-fit black trousers, ivory blouse, and charcoal gray blazer. A nightshade belt accentuated her narrow waist. Jordan pulled out a pair of shoes that she had yet to wear. They matched perfectly. The shoes had unique dark ridges that gave them a crocodile sort of pattern, and their black heels added a touch of class. Diana didn't mind that they were a half-size too large. They were quite comfortable.

"Now, let's add the final touches." Jordan ran into her closet. "Aha! This will do the trick."

She came out with her favorite cognac satchel bag. Diana immediately shook her head.

"Oh no, no. I can't take something so valuable and that you love so much. That's too much responsibility for my messy life."

"You can and you will." She put the Marc Jacobs bag in Diana's hands and pushed her to the long mirror in the corner of her room. Jordan tapped its side to activate the LED lighting so Diana could enjoy her masterpiece. As Diana tried to take it all in, Jordan unbuckled her auburn watch and wrapped it around her wrist.

Diana shook her head, trying to stop the tears forming. "You can't—"

"Girl, don't cry!" Her obnoxious tone made Diana giggle as she wiped her face.

"You wear it well." Jordan winked at her and gave her a thumbs up. "It will bring you luck. I promise!"

Diana stared at her reflection. For the first time, she started to accept herself as a successful, capable woman. She imagined herself working at the office, providing new ideas to the editor while writing her own novels during her free time. She just stood there, smiling at the thought of living the life that she always dreamed of. She didn't realize that Jordan had disappeared until what was likely much later.

After Jordan went to work, Diana had no choice but to face the music. She had to read the next chapter. Otherwise, she would get sucked in against her will again. She couldn't control the fidgeting in her legs. Her voice shook, too. "All right . . . It's now or never. Man, I really don't want to do this!"

She held the book against her chest and closed her eyes. She tried to remember the good time she had with Captain Roger and convince herself that her situation could be enjoyable if she only saw this as a "sexual conquest." It was almost impossible for her to imagine that, though.

She took a deep breath, locked the bedroom door, and found a safe corner to sit in. "I need to get this out of the way. Tomorrow is my interview, and I cannot chance it!"

She opened the book with her eyes closed. She waited, but nothing happened. Then, she came to the realization that she had to flip through the pages. The pages were listed for the first two chapters, but the descriptions were erased. "Huh. I guess I can't go back, only forward." She flipped to the next page. "Here we go!"

Chapter 3: The Knight

On his horse, they rode fast into the wilderness. Nature concealed them from his enemies. His firm arm held her close to his chest. Princess Isabella remained stoic, for she knew the cruelty of men at war . . .

Diana felt that familiar pressure hit her abdomen. She braced herself as she felt the winds building up again. They howled with such intensity, but she did notice a slight difference in the pull. It didn't seem as forceful as the last couple of times. Was it because she was more willing? Either way, it was too late to back out now; she was getting sucked in. She relaxed and let the winds take her. The last thing that she felt in her world was weightlessness in midair.

She opened her eyes when she felt a rocking motion beneath her. She was, in fact, the stereotypical princess dressed in a flowy Cinderella blue gown. Brilliant beams of sunlight pierced through the gray clouds and illuminated the silver patterns on her cloak. The air was thick and smelled of rain. Beneath her, was a black Destrier horse racing to an unknown destination. There were no roads or trails, just trees on top of other trees. Marsh, dead leaves, and dirt covered the earth. Diana screamed for dear life as they rushed down a steep hill, but she was secured by a strong steel arm wrapped around her waist. With his other hand, he jerked the reins to ease his horse.

She screamed as she took over the harness. "Stop!"

"Whoa!" he blurted out.

The horse neighed and reared abruptly. They both slid off and hit the dirt. Diana tried to crawl away from the thrashing horse, but tripped over her dress. As she fell forward, she caught a glimpse of her death as the horse bucked in front of her. Instinctively, she covered her face with her hands, but knew it was not going to be enough protection.

CRACK! The horse had kicked another object. She found the knight blocking her with his long, leather shield. His brute strength pushed the horse back, and it bolted away. He grunted as he caught his breath.

When he turned to face her, Diana grabbed the sides of her gown and took a few steps back. His face was concealed by his steel helm with only small eye slits to see through. He removed his helm and set it down. He waved his long golden locks away from his handsome, clean-shaven face. His sapphire eyes gazed at her with intensity. Under all that armor, she just knew he had a brawny built.

The Narrator took notice of Diana's red face. "Welcome back, Diana. Ready to—"

"Ahh!" she screamed.

Diana lifted the sides of her gown and lunged at the knight, who was also caught by surprise. Before he knew it, she pounced on him and caused them to topple over. From there, she straddled the man and kissed him passionately. She found herself trembling, as it took a lot of confidence to make such a bold move. He showed no protest and, in fact, happily reciprocated.

The Narrator tried to speak again. "Diana, you're—"

"Be quiet!" she grunted as she forcefully pinned the knight's hands against the grass.

As she aggressively unstrapped his armor, the knight spoke up. "I'm not complaining."

"How do you take this damn thing off?" she demanded.

The knight grinned and then quickly assisted her. "Well, I wasn't expecting this," he chuckled.

She yanked her cloak from her shoulders and tossed it aside. With another grin, he wrapped his arms around her waist and flipped positions. Her back fell gently against the grass as he held the back of her head with one hand and cupped her backside with his other. He leaned his head against hers, their noses barely touching. His deep blue eyes looked into hers with curiosity.

"Are you sure?" he whispered.

Diana blushed as she caressed the sides of his face. She pulled him closer and pressed her lips against his.

"Very well." He smirked as he ripped the lace off of her dress with his brutish hands. His kisses traveled down her neck to her breasts. Diana gasped as she wrapped her fingers in his long, golden locks.

She could hear The Narrator speaking quietly—"Suit yourself!"—but she chose to ignore him again. The sarcastic tone in his voice admitted defeat. So, he sat back and allowed them to fulfill their lustful desires.

After the moment passed, they just laid there, still partially clothed. She rested her head on his chest as he entwined his fingers into her brown, flowy hair. Both were still out of breath from their ardent performance. Diana laughed at herself. *I can't believe I thought I wasn't going to enjoy this. As a matter of fact, this was the best sex I've ever had.* She blushed as her mind replayed everything that he did to her.

"No regrets," she giggled.

He smiled and grabbed her hand to kiss it. "I must say," he chuckled, "I really wasn't—"

"Scoundrel!" a loud yell echoed in the distance. They looked up and noticed another knight racing down the hill on a white steed, holding what appeared to be a giant sword. Diana threw her cloak back on and took cover behind a large rock. Her companion, still half-naked, readied his sword and prepared for battle. The other knight, clad in full battle armor, climbed off his horse and charged at him. It was a duel to the death!

Diana shouted at the sky. "Narrator! What gives? I completed my task! Do I have to stick around for this?"

He laughed. "You didn't complete your task."

Her eyes widened. "What do you mean? I had sex! The chapter should be over!"

"I tried to tell you, but you wouldn't listen!"

"Go on then," she gulped. "Tell me."

"You fell for the adversary."

Diana froze. "Y-you, you mean I had sex with . . . with—"

"The *bad guy*!" he chortled. "The knight fighting him was supposed to rescue you and make love to you!"

"The chapter was called *The Knight*! How the hell was I supposed to know?" she shouted. "Am I blind or was this man not dressed as a knight?"

The blond knight smirked as his sword clashed with his opponent's. He overheard her question from afar.

"My intent was to steal you away . . . to be held for ransom," he grunted as he pressed forward with his sword. "Though now, it seems that I got the better end of the deal. You're mine."

Diana crossed her arms and narrowed her brows. "Oh, hell no."

The heroic knight punched him in the face and knocked him down. He swung his sword once more, but the blow was dodged. "You defiled my lady's honor?" he yelled with fury. "I shall kill you!"

Diana looked up with pleading eyes and spoke with a softer tone. "Okay, how do I fix this?"

"You need to mend the relationship with your lover and complete the chapter," The Narrator told her. "If you're not in the mood, there is nothing that I can do for you."

"What?!" Diana shrieked.

"You better hope that he wins and takes you back because there is no other way out of this chapter."

The worried look on Diana's face amused him, but he also wanted to lighten the mood a bit. "By the way . . ."

Diana perked up. "Yeah?"

"How did you do that thing with your back and your leg?"

"Oh, shut up," she screeched. "You perv!"

She needed a plan to ensure her rescuer would win. She looked around for any weapons nearby. She was in complete panic mode.

"There's nothing here other than . . ." She looked up the hill. "Rocks!"

If Diana was confident in anything, it was her impeccable aim. She smiled as a quick memory invaded.

She was grateful for all the months that she participated in Jordan's company baseball league. At first, she wasn't so interested, but Jordan eventually persuaded her. Being on her team was just what she needed in her reclusive life. After many practices, it was clear she was the team's best pitcher. Diana twisted Tom's arm to join, but he rarely attended.

She grabbed a few sizable stones and ran toward the men. She threw the first one.

"Ouch!" the bad guy wailed as he grabbed his left shoulder.

"Haha!" Diana cheered.

She threw the other, straight to his gonads! The man fell to his knees and gasped for air as she danced with victory. The Narrator laughed and cheered with her.

"Great aim! I'm actually impressed."

Even though she couldn't see her hero's expression through his helm, he must have been intrigued. Without further thought, he swung his sword with great strength and sliced his enemy's head clean off! Diana froze as she watched the head roll into a nearby stream, followed by a large trail of blood.

"Umm . . . what just happened?" she whispered.

"Your man won," The Narrator said plainly.

The knight sheathed his sword and ran to her. She held her breath, fearing what was to come. He took off his helm and dropped it beside him. He was indeed as handsome as the last. The sun shone over his long, braided hair, revealing different shades of red and brown. His hazel eyes reminded her of autumn—brown and beautiful with specks of gold. Before she could speak, he knelt before her on one knee and lowered his head. There was sadness in his voice.

"Forgive me, Princess." His brows furrowed as his voice began to shake. "Had I come sooner, he wouldn't have . . . had his way."

A part of her wanted to tell him the truth. Guilt weighed on her conscience. His opponent did not force himself on her. It was more like the other way around. *This is just a stupid story. Fiction, nothing more. Besides, the man kidnapped me and then claimed me as his—and who knows how the story would have really ended? Nope, I'm not gonna go there. Not gonna allow myself to feel bad. Might as well "go with it."*

"He didn't," she told him softly.

He lifted his head and met her gaze with confusion.

"He lied. He almost had his way with me. If it wasn't for your valiant rescue . . ."

The knight let out a deep sigh of relief.

"You may rise, Sir Knight."

After he lifted himself from the ground, she threw herself over him in a tight embrace. His eyes widened while his mouth hung open.

"Princess," he whispered.

Diana lifted her head from his beating chest and gazed into his kind eyes. "Thank you for rescuing me."

His eyes softened as he pressed his forehead against hers. "Regardless, my heart, my arm, my sword will forever be yours."

She could feel the blood rushing into her cheeks. She was speechless, "Umm . . . thank you."

With one hand, she wiped a tear from the corner of his eye. His hand gently held her wrist and guided her palm to his lips. His intense gaze never left hers. Her other hand slid up from his chest armor to the side of his neck. She smiled as she lifted her heels. He leaned forward, and his lips brushed against hers. His kiss nearly melted her as their hearts ignited a fiery passion. She gasped when they stepped apart.

He spoke with urgency. "We must conceal ourselves. If the court finds out—"

Diana pressed her fingers against his quaking lips before she kissed them again. She whispered softly into his ear, "Take me."

He caressed the sides of her waist as his strong lips conquered hers. His firm hands slid their way down and lifted her by her bottom. Diana gasped as she found her legs already wrapped around him. His husky voice made her arms tremble around his neck. "I'll take us somewhere safe."

He lifted her to his horse and positioned himself behind her. He held onto the reins with one hand and pressed her against him with his other. They rode past the trees, through the forest, and to the back end of his stone-walled manor, where a few servants lined up to greet him.

"Welcome back, m'lord." They all bowed and kept their heads down. Two of them unstrapped pieces of his armor until he was down to a simple black tunic. Another took his horse, shield, and sword.

An older maid approached Diana and tensely bowed before her. "Princess—"

Diana bent over to help her up. "Please rise."

"Not a word of this." His abrupt voice startled his servants. "I will deliver the princess to the king myself."

He turned to face his maid and spoke with a softer tone. "While Princess Isabella is at our estate, she'll be receiving our greatest hospitality. See to it that she is taken care of."

He smiled as he saw Diana clutching the cloak that barely covered her ripped garments. He reached for the coin purse that hung under his leather belt and placed it into his maid's hands. "Find a suitable gown for her as well."

The staff took a large step back before they bowed their heads once more. With a single nod, he directed a younger maid to take Diana into the home. She linked arms with hers and guided her upstairs to his chamber, where a fireplace, a platter of food, and a warm bath were readied for her. Diana sat in the wooden tub while she rested her head over her knees, holding them against her chest. The warm water became murky from the gray soap that was tossed in. Its lavender, thyme, and sage scent soothed her. The young maid smiled at her as reached for the sponge. Diana lifted her head from her knees and quickly retrieved it before she could.

"I got it!"

The maid backed herself into a corner and lowered her head. "My apologies, your highness!"

Diana waved her hands in front of her and nervously giggled. "No, don't apologize! I appreciate your help!"

The maid's eyes widened due to the unusual kindness as Diana spoke once more.

"I just enjoy cleaning myself . . . alone, if you don't mind."

"Oh." She nodded as she slowly backed out the door. "Is there anything else I can do for you?"

"I'm fine," Diana assured her with a smile.

The moment the servant left the room, Diana let out a long sigh of relief and sunk her head under the water. *What have I gotten myself into now? Why the delay? I need to get out of here.* A loud yet familiar voice made its way into the room.

"Are you all squeaky clean?"

Diana lifted her head and looked around, then let out another sigh when she realized who it was.

"Oh, it's you," she murmured. "I can't believe I can hear your voice underwater."

"Well," he chuckled, "let's just say in other chapters that may be helpful."

"Are you serious?"

"I gotta say, Diana . . ."

"Yeah?"

"You sure know how to get yourself out of sticky situations. That was an amazing act you put on for Sir Aldric."

"That's his name?" Diana folded her lips and rubbed her tongue behind them. She could still taste the sweetness of his kiss. She didn't want to admit it, but she felt a little bad about lying to him. "Let's just say that I had to learn very quickly how to get out of 'sticky situations.' I should have listened to you. I'll do better next time."

The Narrator's playful voice softened with concern. "You wanna talk about it? We have a little time."

She took a deep breath in and then slowly let it out. "For as long as I can remember, I always felt that I had no control over my life. I lost my job. My boyfriend of eight years cheated on me and kicked me out. Umm, let's see . . . I'm basically homeless. And oh yeah, now I'm cursed!"

She chuckled through tears. "Like, why is it so hard for me to find happiness?"

"Hmm," he mused. "Damn. That really sucks!"

"I *know*!" She sank her mouth underwater, bubbles from her drowning shriek rising and popping at her face.

"Diana, I'm really sorry."

She rolled her eyes. *Is he seriously being genuine?*

"I'm not a therapist by any means."

Oh, lord. Here we go.

"But," he added, "I know that you can't *find* happiness. You can only *create* happiness for yourself."

She wiped a tear from her cheek and cracked a small smile. "That's beautiful."

"I know."

"For a second, I thought you were gonna tell me that I needed therapy."

"You fuckin' do," he said blatantly.

Her eyes narrowed. "Really?"

"Diana, this may be hard for you to believe, but I really enjoy your company."

She scrunched her nose. "What?"

"I'm trying to be serious here."

Her hands caressed the water above her legs. She looked down at the small waves between her fingers. "All right, keep going," she murmured.

"I know you view this book as a curse, but with me as your narrator—as your guide—I can help you create the happiness that you desire. Of that, I can most definitely assure you."

His kind words pulled her out of her pit of misery. Another smile cracked from her lips.

"What was your ex's name?"

"Tom," she sniffled as she wiped her nose with her hand. "He said I was the worst lay of his life."

"Well, from what I've seen, that's not the case. I say fuck him. As a matter of fact, unfuck him! I need you to say that!"

"Un . . . fuck him?"

"Yes, Diana! And if you think the adversary of this chapter was good enough in the sack, then this Tom of yours must have been extremely bad!"

She held onto the sides of her tub and pulled herself up a bit. "You know what, you're right. Unfuck him!"

"Louder, damn it!" he cheered.

Diana rose to her feet as water splashed everywhere. She grinned as she raised her fist to the air and yelled, "Unfuck him!"

"Good." His voice then softened with caution. "Sir Aldric's coming in five, four, three, two, one."

Her knight opened the door to find a beautiful, naked goddess standing before him. Water dripped from her body as she stepped out of the tub. She walked toward him with a small yet inviting smile. Her wet hands brushed up against his bare chest and found their way to the base of his neck. She tilted her head and leaned forward, meeting his mouth halfway. Her breath mingled with his as she whispered to him.

"I'm ready for you."

His hands gripped her hips and pulled her against him. His strong, passionate kiss sent waves of pleasure that awoken a raging storm within her. Within seconds, she pounced on him and wrapped her legs around his waist. He managed to hold his balance and smirked as he carried her to his bed.

His left arm kept her secured beneath him as his roaming tongue traveled to the peaks of her breasts. Diana silently gasped, suppressing any sounds of pleasure that tried to escape. She began to lift herself, but his strong hand gently pressed her chest back down. The side of his smooth face brushed against hers.

"Lie down, Princess," he whispered, then kissed below her ear. "I shall do all the work and see you properly satisfied. I'm going to make you cry out my name."

She wrapped her arms around his head and stared to the ceiling with a brow raised. "Umm?"

The Narrator whispered. "Sir Aldric!"

She nearly giggled. *Oh yeah, right.*

After they were finally spent, she laid herself over him and brushed her fingers through his chest hair. She couldn't help but wonder about him.

"Sir Aldric?"

"Hmm?"

She bit her bottom lip. "Were you just as satisfied?"

He turned to his side and rested his head on his hand. He moved a strand of hair from her face and chuckled at her absurd question. "If I could choose, I would have you for a lifetime. I'm already bursting at the thought of it."

She giggled as blood rushed back into her cheeks. "Well, that's good to know."

"In fact," he moved closer to her, "let's have another go at it."

The Narrator had to intervene. "Not to freak you out, but you will see a guiding light outside his chamber door in a few seconds."

"Huh? Now?" she murmured.

"Don't worry, though. He won't be able to see it or the portal. None of them will. Just open the door and follow the light."

Sir Aldric tilted his head and leaned in for another kiss. "Of course. We have time before I deliver you home."

Diana rolled her eyes, "Hang on. Bookmark!"

The chapter paused and everything around her froze. Diana covered herself with a blanket and climbed out of the bed.

"So, you're telling me that the portal is out that door? Like, now I have to make a run for it?"

"Sorry, I don't place them. I just find them."

She pursed her lips. "Fine. Can I do it now while I'm using this bookmark?"

"Nope."

"Great."

"You'll be fine. Just tell him you must excuse yourself. Or, I guess you can run away like you did last time. That was fun to watch."

"Okay. I think I know what to say."

"Great! Resuming in three, two, one."

Sir Aldric lifted himself from where he laid. "That's strange. I didn't see you leave the bed."

"I need to be excused for a moment, if that's all right?"

"Where do you need to go?"

"Umm," she started to back up toward the door. "I need to use the toilet."

He looked puzzled. "The what?"

The Narrator laughed. "Must I correct you on time periods again?"

Diana held a finger up. "Oh! I meant the privy chamber!"

Sir Aldric chuckled as he motioned for her to look in the corner near him. "Your chamber pot awaits."

Diana cringed as her hand reached for the door.

"Princess?" He raised a brow. "Is everything all right?"

"Oh, *hell no.*"

She clasped the blanket around her and ran out the door. A glowing arrow pointed for her to keep running down the corridor. "Princess, wait!" She could hear Sir Aldric yelling, but she refused to look back. The Narrator, however, gave her a full play-by-play.

"Oh, would you look at that! A naked man on the run! Diana, you better pick up the pace!"

At the end of the hall, she found that familiar flickering green light glowing intensely. "There it is!" she screamed.

"That is not where the privy is!" Sir Aldric yelled back.

It then expanded into a giant orb before her. *Only a few feet away!* She turned her head and found Sir Aldric's hand nearly grasping her arm. Before he could get a grip, she collided with the portal as it opened.

Diana fell back into the corner of her bedroom floor, fully clothed in her comfy yoga pants and sweatshirt. The green light with shimmering golden flecks was sucked into the book as it closed on its own. For a moment, she stood in silence, absorbing everything that happened.

"That was actually fun," she said to herself. *The Narrator was right. I can create my own happiness . . . and who's to say I can't be the heroine in every love story?*

She waggled her brows and grinned.

Chapter 12

The following morning was blissful. Diana woke up feeling more rested. The pleasant scent of freshly brewed coffee and waffles drew her to the kitchen. Jorden stood behind her black quartz island, slicing strawberries.

"Hey, gorgeous. One waffle or two?"

Diana smiled. "Can I have three?"

"Absolutely," she grinned. "Coffee is ready. I'll meet you at the table as soon as I finish."

"Thank you."

Diana poured herself a cup before she sat down. She pulled out the laptop, but couldn't seem to concentrate on the interview questions they practiced the day prior. She replayed Chapter 3 in her head, losing count of how many times she had climaxed. When Jordan walked in with their breakfast, she couldn't help but notice Diana's flushed cheeks and the twinkle in her eyes. Her perverted giggled woke Diana up from her daydream.

"You must have had a good night," Jordan teased.

Diana blushed even more. "What do you mean?"

She sipped her coffee with slanted eyes. "Heck, I would, too. You must have needed that release, lefty."

Diana sunk into her seat as her friend laughed. "Let's just change the subject!"

"There is something going on with you, though." Jordan pondered a bit. "Can't put my finger on it."

Diana nervously giggled. "There's nothing going on, I swear."

"Hmm . . . whatever you say."

They gave each other a "serious" look as they sipped their coffee. Diana wanted to tell Jordan about the book, but she either wouldn't believe her or she would freak out. Diana also had to be very careful because Jordan had a way of finding things out. If there was one thing Diana could do for her friend, it was to protect her.

While Jordan got ready for work, Diana secretly added her "sex days" into her calendar. On her phone, she marked the entire week with red heart emojis. She hoped she could perhaps tackle two chapters on Saturday. The very thought of completing two in one day seemed like a lot at first, but Diana felt she could handle it, especially after her last performances. Bandit tilted his head as he observed her obnoxious giddiness.

Two hours before the interview, Diana got herself ready and posted a picture of herself on social media. The last time she was online, she was spying on Tom. In her new post, she smiled with confidence and imagined herself being successful, living her new, actually fabulous life. A small part of her hoped the photo would catch Tom's eye and show him what he was missing. She *did* feel special for a change. Did she want him back, though? Or did she simply want to pull him in only to deny him a second chance? She didn't know for sure. For now, she just wanted him to look at her picture.

Moments later, her phone rang out the unpleasant yet familiar tune of Beethoven's *Symphony No. 5*. Diana sighed as her thumb hovered over the Answer button. The Caller ID read Lena, her mother's first name. Since the breakup, Diana had avoided Lena's countless phone calls and text messages. Her mother had the tendency to make matters worse. Every time Lena called, Diana felt anxious, especially if the calls were video chats. Flashbacks of her stressful childhood hit her all at once. Even though her parents never separated, she didn't consider them a close-knit family.

***

Lena's main focus was satisfying her abusive husband, Charles. She put everything in her life on hold to appease him, waiting on him hand and foot. No matter how spotless the house was or how well she cooked, it was never enough. He always found a flaw, some reason to stir up unnecessary arguments and quench his drunken rage. There would always be a reason to belittle and abuse her. *Sound familiar?* Diana learned quickly to stay out of it as much as possible.

When she was sixteen, she wanted to call the police after witnessing her father punch her mother, but Lena talked her out of it. That night, Charles eavesdropped on their conversation and beat Diana severely. He threatened to kill her if she even tried to get help; her mother just sat back and watched without showing any sympathy. She learned that her mother loved being his victim. When Diana went to school the next day, nobody asked her how she got all those bruises. She felt more alone than ever. That's how she met Tom. He was the only one who seemed to care after noticing, and he offered to walk her home every day after school. From there, their relationship grew.

Earlier on, Tom was a kind and caring boyfriend. The only fury he showed was on the ice during hockey games. And, of course, being in a relationship with the team's captain made the rest of Diana's high school years a breeze. She would always tag along during his practices and games. She went out with him, his friends, and even their girlfriends. Tom did whatever it took to get her out of that toxic house.

He was her sanctuary. When she needed to go home, he would always make sure she felt safe. When she needed an escape, he would sneak her out of the house. After they graduated, they moved out of their small town and to the big city, far away. He told her that she could start fresh and be anything that she wanted to be. As much as she tried, she couldn't let go of the past. Not knowing how or why he changed killed her.

***

She took a deep breath and answered the call. "Hi, Mom."

"Diana! It's about time! Why haven't you been answering?"

"Sorry." She bit her lip. "I was just busy."

"So busy that you couldn't answer your own mother? You weren't too 'busy' when you posted a provocative picture online," she argued.

Diana's frustration grew. "Mom, they're interview clothes."

Lena's disappointment was obvious. "So, I take it that you and Tom are no longer together? I saw his post."

She rolled her eyes. "Yeah. We broke up."

Lena sighed. "Diana, what did you do?"

The question shocked her. "What did *I* do? Are you *kidding* me?"

"He is such a nice boy."

"Mom, he cheated on me and then kicked me out."

"So, I take it you're moving back to Belding?" Her mother pretended to sound excited. "Your bedroom is the same as you left it."

"No, I'm Jordan's new roommate."

Diana heard Charles laugh in the background. "So, she's wearing her clothes now? Dyke."

"Mom, I need to go."

The sound of her father's voice triggered her enough to hang up. She felt her confidence deteriorating. She immediately went online and deleted her post before anyone could comment on it. She even questioned whether going to the interview was a good idea. She sat at the edge of the bed and eyed the book.

"How could someone go from a hundred to zero in a matter of seconds? At least your characters are fond of me."

She forced herself to laugh. Humor was often her coping tactic of choice. She didn't want Jordan's efforts to go to waste. "I guess I'll go for practice. Maybe I'll learn something . . . or maybe I'll make a complete ass out of myself."

Chapter 13

Diana was scheduled to meet a man by the name of Jerry Wilcox on the first floor of the building, where The Welcome Reader had a coffee shop for its employees and the public. He was an older gentleman who looked to be in his early seventies. To Diana, he met the criteria of one of those "cute old men," with his thick white mustache and gray ivy cap. His kind, brown eyes were welcoming. They sat at a table and placed their orders.

"Go ahead, Diana," he said, deferring to his guest.

"Hot mocha with coconut milk, please," she told the server.

"Same for me, Samantha."

Jerry turned to Diana, staring at her intensely as he rubbed the corners of his moustache. "I firmly believed that coffee says a lot about a person's disposition."

The horror on Diana's face must have amused him. "Don't worry!" he added quickly. "I'm just messing with you. I'm simply curious what it tastes like."

Diana let out a sigh of relief and smoothed her hair. "You had me there," she chuckled.

"Let's get started, shall we?"

"Sure."

The interview lasted for an hour. In the beginning, he asked her questions about her personal life, her education, and why she was interested in the position. It appeared they had a lot more in common than she thought. He grew up in a small town, went off to college, and then pulled extra shifts at a coffee shop while building his writing empire.

"When I was your age, I wrote my first novel and learned a lot about the editing and publishing process. It was a major learning experience for me, and that is why I built this company—to help others succeed. All I can really tell you is never give up on what you're passionate about."

Jerry took the first sip of his coconut mocha, and his eyes lit up. "I didn't think this was going to be delicious, by the way. I was wrong."

She was relieved when he asked questions similar to what she had practiced with Jordan. She watched his facial expressions every time he wrote in his folder. His constant smiling gave her hope, but he had to be blunt about her lack of experience in the field. It sounded like her two-year internship wouldn't be enough.

Going over her previous job description also likely didn't make her stand out from the other hopefuls. She did make him laugh with some of her claim stories, though. He was willing to listen to what she had to say, and they connected over her passion for writing. He skimmed through his packet to check whether anything had been missed.

"Ah, yes." His smile widened. "I meant to bring this up from the start. I received a letter of recommendation from Sherry Whitfield."

Diana had no idea who he was talking about. "Sherry—"

"Hmm, I'm very impressed," he continued as he glanced at the letter. "She had a lot of nice things to say about your work."

Diana refrained from asking who Sherry was. She just went with it. "Oh . . . well that was sweet of her."

"Well, I think that's it." He set his folder down and smiled. "I will consider your application. Do you have any questions for me?"

"Yes," Diana said. "When should I hear back regarding the position?"

"We have four other people to interview, but you should hear back from us within two weeks."

"Perfect." She smiled back. "Thank you so much for your time. It was seriously a pleasure speaking with you."

"And you as well."

They shook hands and parted ways. On the way out, Diana fanned her face with her hand as she panicked in silence. When she felt more centered, she pulled out her phone. *Who the heck is Sherry Whitfield?* Multiple names and professions pulled up on Google, but none looked familiar. She couldn't find much on social media, either. Even when she filtered her search, nothing pulled up in her location. Diana shrugged her shoulders. *Maybe it's someone from my old writing class? Or perhaps an old professor who doesn't use technology as much?*

When she made it back home, she threw on Jordan's workout gear and met up with her and Bandit at the gym. It was shoulder day—their favorite. They discussed the interview while doing upright rows and Arnolds. Jordan was excited to hear all about it, while Bandit just laid beside the bench and observed their every move.

Diana cut into the middle of her story. "By the way, do you know who Sherry Whitfield is?"

"Nope."

"Huh." Diana pondered some more.

Jordan shrugged her shoulders. "I need the rest of the story, sis!"

"It went so well. The experience thing obviously hurt me, but other than that, we had a great conversation. And he really likes my signature coffee!"

"Ooh, nice!"

"Yep. Either way, at least the worst is over. Now I just wait for the rejection."

"Or the job offer!" Jordan interjected. "by the way, why did you delete your post? You looked so pretty."

Diana bit her lip. "My mom called."

"Lena, the queen of drama and destruction," she mocked.

"Yeah, she called the way I was dressed 'provocative.' To top it off, my dad called me a dyke."

Jordan's brows narrowed. "Umm, what the hell? Why would he even call you that?"

"Well, I told them that I was living with you. And—"

Jordan slammed down her barbell. "So that means that we're a couple now? I would like for him to say that to my face."

A nervous laugh escaped Diana's mouth. "I'm sure he's very intimidated by you."

Jordan chuckled as she picked up a heavier weight. "I wish he would. Fucking dickhead."

It was obvious that her friend was pissed. From their workouts together, Diana noticed that Jordan never had a problem with receiving compliments from women or even being flirted with by them. But when it came to being called a lesbian, especially in an offensive way, she would get infuriated. "A woman can be successful and dominate in the workplace without being a lesbian. We don't all belong at home with a bunch of kids," she would say.

In a way, Diana could relate. *Before I met her, I was freakishly skinny. Everyone assumed that I was sick.* Memories of all the times they shared at the gym came back to her—the rigorous training, new and necessary pains, strict diet plans, and recording results every month.

Of course, there was also dealing with Tom's body-shaming. *I have changed a lot . . . and for the better.*

Jordan glanced at the mirror in front of them and noticed Diana's smile. "What's so funny?"

Diana turned to face her. "You know, if it weren't for you, I wouldn't have these amazingly capped shoulders and a butt."

Jordan chuckled again. "You did all the work, not me."

"But," she persisted, "you showed me how to do it and you always encouraged me to keep going. I love how I look now, so thank you."

"Well, I—"

"And . . . I think people who judge us based on how we look are really insecure. If we were lesbians, we would make the best couple, don't you think?"

Jordan looped an arm around her. "Damn straight."

"Damn it, we are basically a couple," Diana joked.

Later that evening, Jordan's phone interrupted dinner. She excused herself from the table. Diana was obviously fascinated and tried listening in on the conversation. *This must be her secret lover!*

Jordan waved her hand for Diana to back off.

"It's work," she whispered with a smirk. She took the phone into her office and shut the door.

Sure, it is. Diana took a huge bite from her plate and quietly moved to the other side of the door. Changes in Jordan's volume as she moved around jolted Diana from her spot, and then she'd swiftly return.

"Wait a minute," Jordan laughed. "You're telling me that after all these years, you finally got—"

Diana softly pressed her ear against the door.

Jordan gasped. "Aww! So, he went to your office and asked you out? This is amazing! Why are you panicking?"

Okay, who is she really *talking to?*

"It went well. Fingers crossed." After a few seconds, Jordan's voice softened, "Oh, okay. . . . Okay. . . . You need me to fly there? When? . . . I see. . . . Well, it's not a problem for me! Seriously, take this time for yourself. Enjoy the moment. You really deserve it," Her giggling persisted. "You're welcome."

Diana heard her voice approaching the door again and made her escape back to the kitchen table with fork in hand. Jordan smirked as she waltzed out of the office.

"How much did you hear?"

Diana chuckled as she twisted her spaghetti around. "Not enough for me to know—"

"Ha! I told you it was work!"

"So, does someone have a date and is panicking?"

Jordan nodded. "My boss. She's been having a difficult time expressing her feelings to an old flame of hers. I kinda persuaded her to make the first move."

"Ooh!" Diana's eyes widened. "Well, that's so sweet. I hope it works out."

"Me too, which is why I need your help."

Diana perked up. "Oh? What do you need?"

Jordan sighed. "I need you to watch Bandit for a week. I'm taking my boss's assignment so she can have the week off."

"I can do that, no problem. When and where are you going?"

"I need to leave for Denver tomorrow morning at eight sharp. I'll be back on Tuesday."

Diana smiled and nodded. *Next Tuesday? Seven days—plenty of time to read.*

Jordan interrupted her thoughts with another smirk. "And don't worry. We're still gonna make it to baseball. You better bring A-game!"

Diana forgot that tryouts for the new season were coming up. She would be on Jordan's roster regardless, but she didn't want to disappoint her.

"You can count on me!" Diana squealed.

That next morning, after Jordan left, Diana rushed back into her room to retrieve the book. The rush of excitement tickled her. *How many chapters can I finish in a week without any interruptions? Will I make it all the way to the end? Who else am I going to sleep with?*

The thrill directed her focus away from Tom, the editing position, her parents, and the rest of the bullshit. She knew that she had an opportunity that no one else had, and it was for her and her alone.

Chapter 14

Diana received a call from Jordan as soon as her plane landed Tuesday. As promised, Diana didn't forget tryouts and was looking forward to showing everyone her amazing pitching skills. She agreed to meet her at the field with Bandit to set everything up. Was she on time? Absolutely not. Not only was it two days before Christmas, but Diana had just finished another chapter, making it fifteen in total. That was double the amount that she had initially planned.

Finding a good outfit to wear was challenging. Since Diana didn't have much of her own clothing, she succumbed to Jordan's closet. All of her activewear was pretty revealing. Of course, at this point, Diana didn't care as much. Being naked most of the time lately probably had something to do with that. She picked out a rose-colored sports bra that crisscrossed in the back. The front lifted her breasts as the keyhole center revealed where they met. She paired it with high-waisted, black spandex pants and knee-high gray socks. She let her long, wavy hair down before she put Jordan's Arsenal FC cap on.

As she waited for the stop light to turn green, Jordan texted.

Jordan: Diana! You better not be late! I'm counting on you!

> **Diana:** *Two stops away! Don't worry, babes!*

With another swipe of her finger, she resumed her playlist. She giggled as "Slip of the Lip" by Ratt blasted from her speakers.

The air was crisp and the sun was out, which was unusual for late December in Detroit, but it was perfect for baseball. As Diana pulled in, she noticed more vehicles. *Wow! Way better than last year. I better bring my A-game for sure.*

She could pick out some of the players. Last season's team members showed up in their practice uniforms, which were gray triple-striped pants, white baseball tees with orange sleeves, and orange caps. Newer members wore regular activewear. Diana tried counting with her eyes. About forty people showed up to try out for the Metro Monarchs.

From a distance, she saw Jordan pacing the field with her phone in hand. Diana got out of her Versa and looped her arm around Bandit. With her other hand, she swung her bat over her shoulder as she approached the field.

"Yoohoo," Diana called.

Jordan turned her head and give her the biggest grin she had ever seen. "Oh my God," Jordan yelled and then began cat-calling her out loud enough for everyone to hear. Her teammates joined in, making Diana blush and giggle. She set Bandit down, still holding his leash, as she dramatically dropped her booty, almost touching the sand. Jordan and her team cheered louder and started to clap.

"Stop . . . stop," Diana giggled as she waved her hand.

Jordan ran up to her with excitement. "What did I miss?"

"Huh? Nothing," Diana smiled. "How was your trip?"

"It was great, but not that important! Don't change the subject! Look at yourself! You're smokin' hot!"

Diana chuckled. "Well, thank you!"

Jordan's grin was persistent. "Did you get the job? Did you meet someone? What the hell did I miss?"

"Well, not yet! I've just been reading a lot and working out and—"

A loud exhaust interrupted their conversation. Diana could feel her heart pounding. It was a red Honda Accord she was quite familiar with. She shut her eyes tightly and reopened them. *No! This can't be happening.* Oh, but it was happening.

Tom and Gwenyth stepped out of his car. To make matters worse, Gwenyth wore Diana's team uniform and had tied the T-shirt to show off her pierced navel. Jordan stepped in front of Diana with her jaw clenched and her arms wrapped in front of her.

"Don't worry, I'll handle this."

"Jordan." Diana reached out, but it was too late.

Her best friend met the couple halfway across the field, but she could still hear them talking.

"You two are not welcome here. Please leave."

"Ooh, you were right about her attitude," Gwenyth snickered.

Tom smirked at Jordan. "But we're here for the tryouts."

Jordan spoke firmly. "Oh, so now you're interested?"

Tom laughed as he pulled up the contract on his phone. "This is your contract, yes? It says that everyone has the right to play. I mean, we can leave if you're willing to deal with the consequences."

Jordan called his bluff with a chuckle. "You seriously have the balls to file a suit against me?" She pulled up the contract on her phone as well. "It also says that you both need to fill out an injury waiver, which takes up to twenty-four hours to—"

Jordan's phone chimed twice. She paused to read her screen, then realized that she had just received their completed waivers. She pursed her lips and rolled her eyes.

Gwenyth laughed in her face. "You were saying?"

They walked past her to talk with the other members. Jordan immediately turned to face Tom.

"Why are you doing this to Diana? Aren't you satisfied enough?"

"This isn't about her. Gwen loves baseball."

Jordan yelled as she placed her hands over her hips. "You're such a liar and a heartless jerk! You just want to flaunt that slut in front of her. Do you seriously have nothing else better to do?"

"I don't see the problem here," Tom argued playfully. "She's living with you. She's your woman now."

Gwenyth laughed as Tom continued. "It's pretty obvious that you've been crushing on her since you've met her."

Jordan slanted her eyes and smirked at him. "Sure . . . whatever you say."

He tilted his head. "What does that mean?"

With her fingers, she slightly lowered her sunglasses and purposely stared at his crotch. "Nothing."

Diana gulped as she saw Jordan walk toward her with her head still shaking. Jordan's hand touched her shoulder and guided her back into the dugout. "I'm sorry. There's nothing I can do. They're using my contract against me."

Diana returned her gaze with a small smile. "It's really okay. I'm just a bit stunned." *The last time I saw them together was in my bed. God, get over it already!*

"Of course you are," Jordan lowered her head as she spoke in a softer tone. "If you want, you don't have to stick around. I'm not gonna pick them anyway, and you'll always have a spot on this team."

They didn't realize that Tom and Gwenyth were standing behind them until Gwenyth cleared her throat to get their attention.

"I still can't believe he brought his skank to show her off," Jordan whispered. "She has nothing on you. Seriously, Diana, never sell yourself short."

Diana felt the familiar stinging pain behind her eyes. She grabbed Jordan's sunglasses from where she wore them as a headband. "Can I wear these? I forgot mine at the house, and I need to see clearly when I'm pitching."

Jordan grinned. "That's the spirit."

"Are we going to play or what?" Gwenyth snapped.

Tom stepped in front of the best friends. "You heard her. When are we going to start?"

Diana put the sunglasses on and forced a smile.

"What the hell are you smiling at?" he asked scornfully.

Diana remembered Jordan's hilarious move from earlier. Her eyes scanned him from his face to crotch. "Nothing."

He narrowed his brows as the bridge of his nose scrunched. He was about to say something, but was cut off by Jordan.

"All right, you guys!" she yelled to the participants. "We're gonna start with a few warmups! Let's go!"

Everyone ran three laps around the field, did push-ups, sit-ups, jumping jacks, lunges, and jump squats. Jordan increased the rep count, as she wanted Tom and Gwen to feel her wrath. There was a lot of heavy breathing on the field, but this wasn't anything new for Diana. When the warmups were finished, the players partnered up for long throwing, short throwing, and swinging.

After those stations and a five-minute water break, Jordan separated everyone into two teams. Diana found it amusing how Gwenyth retied the front of her shirt every time she passed by. And Tom? That fool couldn't stop staring at his ex. He and Gwen couldn't help but notice something was different, too. Oh, how the tables have turned.

Tom and Gwenyth were on offense, ready to bat. For safety reasons, Jordan didn't want Diana to have much contact with them, so she placed her out in left field.

"Aww, come on! I wanted to show off my pitching," Diana complained. "It's not like Tom was around to see any of it last season anyway. I'll be good!"

"Don't worry," Jordan assured her. "You'll have plenty of time to shine. Honestly, I'm more worried about the dynamic duo over there starting some shit."

"Okay, fine. At least you're in center field so we can still talk."

Tom was second to bat. Baseball was not his sport. His swing was as lousy as his attitude. After the third strike, he tossed his bat petulantly.

"This isn't hockey!" Jordan jeered as Diana laughed.

Gwenyth tried to console him, but it was no use.

"I would like to see you on the ice!" he shouted.

"Aww, somebody's sad," Jordan taunted with an exaggerated crying gesture.

Tom was about to head her way, but Gwenyth pulled him by his arm toward the dugout. Diana was ready to rush over to protect her friend, but Jordan waved for her to remain in position. Other teammates whispered to each other, and Diana's cheeks turned red.

"Man, that guy is psycho."

"How did she put up with him for so long?"

"What is his problem? How embarrassing."

Gwenyth yelled at Tom. "Knock it off!" He sat there with his arms crossed like a four-year-old, and she stomped her foot. After she calmed him down, she grabbed the bat and smiled before entering the diamond.

"Now, watch me smash this," Gwenyth announced.

She made it to home plate, swung the bat over her shoulder, and steadily held her position. She stared at the pitcher solemnly. She hit the first pitch, and it was *gone*! Gwenyth's surprised teammates cheered as she made it to second, then third.

Jordan's jaw dropped as her eyes followed the ball. It was out of the park. "Damn it."

Tom ran out of the dugout with his arms wide open as her foot landed on home base. She jumped on him, legs wrapped around his hips. She kissed him passionately while she wrapped her arms around his neck. He spun her around as they laughed, and Gwen looked over his shoulder to spot Diana. Her smirk made it obvious she wanted to get a rise out of her former coworker.

With the help of Jordan's sunglasses, Gwen didn't see Diana's glossy eyes. She folded in her lips and turned to the side, pretending that her attention was elsewhere, but she could still see how happy they were from the corner of her eye. She thought she had moved on, but it was still too painful to watch. The men who she had been with were fictional, but what she saw in front of her was real. It was the life she once lived. She was starting to feel nauseous as her hands began to tremble.

A few concerned teammates started to approach her. From the looks on their faces, they had a lot of questions. *That's right... I didn't tell them what happened. Well, I certainly can't start now.* Her eyes met Jordan's for help.

Jordan ran up to their friends before they reached Diana. She spoke quietly, but Diana could still hear.

"You guys, now is not the time. It's really up to her to tell you. Just be supportive, okay?" Her friends nodded and muttered something inaudible. After they walked away, Jordan smiled at her and gave her a thumbs up. Diana took a deep breath in and tried forcing a smile as she silently thanked Jordan for the rescue.

About an hour in, the teams swapped positions. Diana and Jordan were up to bat. The other team voted for Gwenyth to pitch, as she bragged that her pitching game was next-level.

"Are you sure you don't want to sit this one out?" Jordan asked as she glared at Gwenyth.

"No, I'm fine. I need to show them I'm fine."

"I don't have a good feeling about this. I swear to God: If she hurts you—"

"I'll be okay. Don't worry."

Jordan nodded with her arms crossed. "Well, if it's intentional, I'll throw her out."

She gave her a half-smile. She kept her sunglasses on to shield her emotions.

Jordan leaned in closer to get a better look at her face. "Are you sure you're okay?"

Diana didn't mean to, but she responded with a rough tone that made her friend flinch. "Yes!"

It was an intense game. Jordan's team was a little behind, but they still had a chance of winning. Unfortunately, Diana was last to bat and had lost all confidence in herself. She wished she would have gone first to sit most of the game out, but it was a last-minute decision that she quickly regretted. And now, the pressure was on. It was up to her to either make or break the game. For a moment, she wished The Narrator was around to humor her. She smiled at the thought of him lurking around, talking in his sexy, sarcastic tone.

She took a deep breath and stepped up to the plate. Batting was not her forte. Before she got in position, she looked to Tom in right field and then at Gwenyth, who was smiling menacingly at her. *They're gonna make fun of me for sure.*

When Diana was ready, Gwenyth sent her first pitch. Diana swung and missed terribly. They laughed, of course. Jordan stood there and shook her head. She gave her friend a little cheer.

"Come on, Diana! You can do it!"

Gwenyth smiled, as she had her next move picked out. Diana gripped tightly onto the handle as she tried to maintain her form. Her arms rattled. Gwenyth covered the ball with her mitt and then took a slide step to throw. She flicked her wrist to create the perfect curveball. Again, Diana swung and missed. The defense jumped up and down as just one strike remained.

Diana looked down at her feet. She wanted to give up, but Jordan called a time-out and jogged toward the plate.

"Girl, try to not load forward as much while swinging. Make sure your hands are kept back while waiting for the ball. You fuckin' got this."

Diana nodded. She took another deep breath after Jordan left. *You got this. You got this. You fucking got this.*

Gwenyth had another trick up her sleeve. She spoke up when she saw Diana's worried face. "Are you gonna cry again? Go on, cry like the little wimp you are."

"Diana, ignore that twat!" Jordan shouted.

Tom dropped his mitt. "Gwen, that's enough!"

For a second, Diana looked at Tom's concerned face. *Wait, why is he getting involved now?* She turned back to the game. *You need to focus! He doesn't matter! She doesn't matter! What matters is you hitting the fucking ball!*

Gwenyth laughed. "Just having some fun, love."

Diana waved the bat over her shoulder as she felt all this hate and anger build up. *Don't lose control. Don't give her that satisfaction!* She imagined having electrifying powers that charged her bat for the final blow, like something out of a *Super Smash Bros.* game. She was ready to swing.

Gwenyth threw hard. Diana swung hard, and everyone heard two hits. The first was when her bat connected with the ball. The second was when the ball connected with Gwenyth's face. The pitcher dropped to her knees and screamed in agony.

Jordan fell to her knees, too. She couldn't hold back her laughter. Diana was stunned. All of her emotions flew out the window. She just stood there, watching Tom and everybody else rush to Gwenyth's aid. All she could hear was high-pitched screaming as blood sprayed from her face.

"We need a towel and some ice," one person yelled.

Another player looked at the pitcher's face. "Yep, it's broken."

What? Diana's eyes widened with horror. *Oh, no! What have I done?* Diana covered her face with her hands, but could see clearly between her fingers. She ran to Gwenyth and Tom to apologize.

"Oh my God! I'm so sorry, Gwen!"

"Shut up! Shut the *fuck* up, you bitch!" Gwenyth screeched. "This is your fault! I'm going to sue you! You're going to pay!"

Diana panicked. "I seriously didn't mean to—"

Jordan quickly intervened. "Sue? For what? You signed the waiver!" Her laughing continued. "Merry Christmas, bitch!"

Oh yeah . . . she's right! Diana's confidence came back in full blast. She courageously finished her sentence and raised her fist to the air. "And happy fuckin' new year!"

Tom grabbed Gwenyth by the shoulders. "We need to take you to the hospital *now*."

"No shit, Sherlock!"

Jordan and Diana laughed as they listened to them argue all the way to his car. As they drove off, Jordan and Diana linked their arms together, spun around, and chanted in victory! The other players didn't understand what was going on until Diana explained the entire story. They all wanted to celebrate Diana's accidental revenge with beer and wings at their favorite sports bar. It was the greatest and most memorable night of her life.

***

It was eleven at night. Diana was wasted, but rightfully so. It had been a long time since she was this happy. Jordan helped her into the passenger seat so she could doze off comfortably on the way home.

"Jordan, I love you."

She smiled. "And I love you."

"Y-you know what?" Diana mumbled.

"Huh?"

"You . . . you're right about a lot of things."

Jordan chuckled. "I know and—"

"No. Shh. I mean about marriage."

Jordan furrowed her brows as she glanced down at her. "And what did I say again?"

"It's *so* overrated."

"Diana, I never said that. What I said was that Tom wasn't the right—"

She cut her off and raised her voice. "I'm fine with *nobody*. I'm going to live my life to the fullest!"

"Yeah? Good for you."

Diana hiccupped. "From now on, I'm going to be like you! Fuck men. Fuck love."

Jordan's hand pressed lightly against Diana's shoulder. She fell back in her seat with her eyes closed, her voice fading as she drifted off to sleep.

"Go to sleep. We'll talk more about this tomorrow, okay?"

"Uh-huh."

Chapter 15

Diana grunted as she pulled the covers over her head. She didn't want to open her eyes. Her phone kept chiming with text messages, and the sound made her ears throb. *I am never drinking again. This time, for sure.* Sudden loud knocking from the front door followed by five quick doorbell rings startled her. She heard Jordan opening the door, followed by a hauntingly familiar voice.

"Well, well, if it isn't Ms. Olympia in her fancy robe."

"Lena."

"Aren't you going to invite me in?"

Jordan sighed heavily. "I guess."

Yup, I need to get up. Diana held her head while she tried dragging her feet to the floor. She could hear her mother tutting around, already stirring up trouble. Jordan's annoyance remained subtle.

"Can I offer you anything to eat or drink?"

"No," Lena said. "I'm here for my daughter. Where is she?"

"She's still asleep."

"Well, wake her up! I need to talk to her!"

"Can't it wait?" Jordan yawned.

Lena's voice grew louder. "Excuse me?"

"It's seven-thirty in the morning." Jordan yawned again. "I need coffee for this."

Diana stepped out of her room as Jordan walked to the kitchen. The natural morning light nearly blinded her. She squinted her eyes at her mother.

"Mom, what are you doing here?"

"What am I doing here?" she yelled. "I've been trying to reach you for days! You haven't answered any of my calls or texts! I was getting worried—"

Diana held her finger up before allowing her mom to finish, then she ran into the bathroom to throw up. As she was ridding the toxins from her system, she could hear her mom yelling at Jordan from all the way in the kitchen.

"What did you do to my little girl? I knew you were a bad influence! Are you just going to sit there and eat your cereal?"

Jordan's mouth was full. "It's my house. If you don't like it, you can leave."

Diana left the bathroom and made her way to the table. Throwing up never felt so good. Her migraine was slowly dissipating. Jordan poured her a glass of water and handed her some aspirin.

"Jordan, can I get a moment alone with her?"

She nodded and headed into her bedroom with Bandit. That was when things got worse.

"Look at yourself, Diana. I'm so disappointed."

Diana took a sip of her water and cleared her throat. "What else is new?"

"You're throwing your life away with these poor decisions!"

"Poor decisions?" Diana shot back. "Do you really want to go there?"

Lena hammered her fist on the table. "Listen to me or you'll regret it!"

"Get on with it then!"

"Don't give me that attitude. I'm only trying to help!"

Diana couldn't wait for the additional criticism. "Go on, Mom. Say your peace."

Lena huffed and puffed as she paced around the room. "You used to be such a pleasant person. Ever since this breakup, you have been going down the wrong path! You have become this mean, condescending, sarcastic, bitter, selfish woman! I don't like it, and it needs to stop!"

"And you got all of this from talking to me for a couple minutes?"

"Let me finish, damn it!" Lena continued. "You don't have a job, you don't have any money, the only friend you have is clearly a bad influence—"

Diana clenched her fists. "You don't know anything about her, Mom! She's been there for me far more than you have!"

Lena took a step back, tears running down her face. "How could you say that? I am your mother."

Her voice shook, but she got the words out. "You . . . you let him beat me. You just sat back and watched."

"That was a long time ago! You need get over it! Your father is—"

"Still abusive," she finished. "Every time you call me, I can hear him! He hasn't changed! You can't tell me how to live my life when you haven't fully lived yours!"

Lena sat at the end of the table. She covered her face with her hands. Diana wasn't finished.

"You gave up everything for this 'man,' and you always let him treat you like shit! You're the one who needs help, not me! You clearly enjoy being his victim, and I can't be around that. I'm done!"

Lena shook her head in disbelief of what she was hearing. "Tom was perfect for you. You need to make this right."

"What? In what way do you think this was my fault? Like I told you before, *he* cheated on *me* and threw me out!"

Lena softened her voice, but it lacked sympathy. She placed her hand on top of her daughter's, but Diana recoiled. "Diana, we all make mistakes. You need to forgive him."

"I can't." She began to cry.

"Deep down, he is a good man. It may be time for you to reflect on the things you did that contributed to his cheating."

Tears stained Diana's cheeks. "The things that I have done?"

"Think of everything that the poor man had to put up with. If you think you deserve better, think again."

"W-what?" she stuttered.

Lena's words struck her deeply. The horror on Diana's face was unmistakable. *Is this really all my fault?* Before she could consider that thought further, pounding footsteps entered the room.

"Lena, get the fuck out of my house!"

Lena clutched her handbag and stared at Diana. "Do you see the monstrosity that you're living with?"

Diana couldn't control her sobs as Jordan yelled again. "You're the monster, Lena . . . and a shitty mother!"

"Jordan, please," Diana begged.

Jordan approached Lena with clenched fists at her sides. Her voice lowered, but she still sounded threatening. "You're fucking white trash, you know that? You pick your scumbag husband over your own child. Then, you tell her that *she* has issues? Go fuck yourself."

Lena backed herself to the front door, never taking her eyes off Jordan. Her host's angry eyes signaled for Lena to leave, but she didn't open the door.

"I took a taxi here . . ."

She glanced at her daughter, who cried over at the edge of the table. "I hope I got through to you. Come back home."

Jordan quickly retrieved her purse and chucked a roll of cash at her. She flinched when it hit her chest. Then without hesitation, she picked it up from the floor and left.

Jordan slammed the door behind her and let out a growl.

Diana rose from her seat. "Jordan, how could you do that?"

She turned to face her friend. "Diana, I had no idea. I had no idea that your father—"

"Don't." She drew back. "I don't want to talk about it."

Jordan reached out to her with pain in her eyes. "Please let me—"

"I don't need your help! I don't need you to fight my battles, either."

"All I was trying to do—"

"You've done more than enough. I can't take it anymore." Diana pressed her palms against her face. "I can't stay here anymore. I'm moving out."

Jordan looked down at herself and rubbed the back of her head with her hand. "I'm really sorry. Please, let's talk this through."

"I accept your apology, but my decision is final. I can't stay here anymore."

Jordan lifted her head with tears forming. "When? Where are you going?"

Diana held her shaking breath in for a moment and then slowly released it. "I don't know yet. I just can't keep relying on you for help. It's wrong, and it's embarrassing for me."

"It's not. It's—"

Diana turned her back and walked to her room before Jordan could continue. She closed the door behind her and crawled back into bed, where she could cry in peace. Never had she felt so ashamed. She wanted to keep her past locked away, fearing what others would think of her, especially her best friend and biggest inspiration. *Jordan has always been there for me—drama after drama—and my stupid fights with Tom. I've never been able to return the favor or give anything back. The only thing I've done was prove how weak I really am. I didn't want her to know about this. Why the hell couldn't I keep my mouth shut?*

The sound of the garage door closing made her pause. Diana stepped out of bed and opened her door. She was about to walk out when she noticed a wrapped Christmas present by her feet along with an envelope that said *I love you* on top. Diana called out for Jordan, but the house was silent. Through the window, she saw her vehicle leaving the driveway. With no time to spare, she rushed outside to apologize.

She wanted to say, "I love you" back, but it was too late. Jordan and Bandit were gone. For how long was to be determined. Diana rubbed her arms with her hands. Flurries of snowflakes floated from the gray sky, and the cold concrete chilled her bare feet. She carried the present into her room and opened the card first.

For your future novels. I hope you love it!

Love,

Jordan, your best friend and soul sister

It was a brand-new laptop. Diana held it close and sobbed once again. *I'm such a bad friend. Maybe leaving would be the best thing for both of us. I need to wise up and handle my own mess from now on.* She looked at the book, but wasn't in the mood.

Chapter 16

The Michigan weather intensified as a massive blizzard took over. It was one degree outside with twenty inches of snow on the ground. On a positive note, Lena couldn't make the drive up again. In the countryside, all the roads were blotted out by snow and ice. Diana had almost forgotten how people survived over there. Most homes had generators and pantries full for upcoming "apocalypses." Diana received a text from her mother, though.

> **Lena:** *I hope you have a Merry Christmas. We love you very much.*

Diana didn't want to respond, but felt compelled to do so.

> **Diana:** *Merry Christmas. Love you too.*

> **Lena:** *We also talked about your situation. We just want you to know that you do have a place here.*

Lena's message left a bad taste in her mouth, so Diana chose not to respond. As she was about to set her phone down, it chimed once more. She sighed heavily as she read her screen.

> **Lena:** *Dad said that he forgives you and that he can hold a waitressing position for you at his work. Rent will only cost half of your pay. Just something to think about.*

The idea of reverting to her old life in Belding made her stomach turn. She didn't want to move back home, but what choice did she have? Her mother was right about her not having a job or income to support herself. Diana wished that yesterday had never happened. *Things were going so great.*

Earlier that morning, she texted Jordan to say she loved her and that she was ready to talk it out. She didn't know how to feel about Jordan's outburst, and she didn't know where it stemmed from, but it seemed they were both in need of a heart-to-heart conversation. Regardless, she didn't want their argument to damage their friendship. Hours later, she still hadn't gotten any response.

Diana put her phone down and made her way to the kitchen. *I didn't eat anything all day. The least I can do is have dinner. Then, I'll come up with a better game plan.* She opened the pantry door, but it was difficult for her to focus. She caught herself staring blankly at the overfilled shelves that held enough cans and small boxes to create at least twenty different recipes. With a long sigh, she shut the door and turned to the freezer. *Frozen TV dinner it is.*

She took the box of frozen ham and mashed potatoes out and slammed it into the microwave. She pressed her fingers against her temples as her elbows held her head from the counter. As much as she tried to fight off her negative thoughts, they still managed to creep their way in.

She inhaled deeply as she felt the back of her eyes burning again. *I went to college, yet accomplished nothing. No job, no income, and apparently, I can't do better than Tom. What did I seriously do to deserve this? At least what I had with him was real. I can't believe that I have practically become dependent on that dumb book. And who was I to ever think that I was special? I'm a no-good, stupid, worthless, broke, piece of crap . . . and a sex addict, at best! Congratulations, Diana. You're a fucking loser.*

She felt an unsettling pain in her chest as she began to sweat and shake. Her breathing intensified, but she couldn't control her tears. She made her way to the living room and laid on the couch. She was losing control. She held onto herself in a fetal position, as if the world was crashing in. For a moment, she hoped for her death. *I would rather die than go back home.*

The microwave beeped several times. After minutes had passed, she still couldn't get herself off the couch. She could feel her spirit breaking. All hope was lost. *I guess that's it then. I already know what I must do.*

A loud knock at the front door broke the silence. Her anxiety was on high alert, but she was going to be furious if Lena found a way there. She quickly wiped her face with her sleeves, but couldn't hide the evidence of her anguish.

She braced herself before opening the door. When she saw who was standing outside, she lost all willpower. She immediately ran into his accepting arms. Tom held her close as she cried deeply into his chest. Hearing his soft voice made her feel even more vulnerable. It was the voice of someone she used to know.

"Diana?" He tightened his embrace and caressed the back of her head. His voice trembled. "What's wrong? What happened?"

She couldn't get out a single word. It was getting more difficult to breathe. Looking at his worried expression revived the memory of when they first met. He helped her back inside, where they sat on the couch. He tried supporting her head, but she couldn't seem to face him. He went to the kitchen for a clean towel to soak in cold water. When he returned, he wiped the burning tears from her face and placed the damp towel behind her neck. The coolness instantly soothed her. He rubbed her back as she held her face. After a minute, he spoke again.

"Diana, whatever is going on, we'll work through it together. Do you trust me?"

She couldn't speak just yet.

He pulled her hands from her face and held them together. "I need you to breathe with me."

She nodded. "Okay."

They practiced deep breathing exercises together. Tom instructed her to hold her breath in for seven seconds and to exhale for eight. He made her do it with him four times. He also made her do the "whoosh" sounds, which eased more tension. She almost wanted to laugh at his exaggerated expressions. When she felt calmer, he encouraged her with simple words.

"Good. You're doing great."

He cupped the sides of her cheeks and kissed her forehead. She was confused. *Why is he being so nice and caring suddenly?* When he met her gaze, she could tell he had something to say, too. Tom moved his hands around to her shoulders. "Tell me what's going on."

Every time she tried to explain herself, her emotions would take over. Surprisingly, Tom was more patient than ever. He encouraged her to speak slowly so he could better understand her.

When she was ready, she told him everything from the day before. She told him about Lena's unwanted visit and how she triggered Jordan. That part actually made him laugh. She told him about their fight after her past was brought up, about moving out, and about possibly living back with her parents for a while. Tom then understood her panic attack. He sighed deeply before he spoke.

"Diana, I cannot . . . Let me rephrase that. I *will not* allow you to move back with your parents."

She stared at his disappointed face. "Well, what choice do I have, Tom? I lost my job, I haven't heard back about my interview or from any of the other places that I applied to, I only have eighty-two dollars to my name, I ruined the only friendship I had, and—"

Tom cut her off. "You do have a choice. You can move back with me."

"What?" Diana nearly tipped over the couch. "Tom, I can't! We can't!"

"Why? Because of everything that happened?"

"Yes. And regardless, it will make things even more complicated in your relationship with Gwen."

He shook his head as his eyes veered to the ceiling. He tried forcing a smile, but Diana knew he was really hurting inside. Before she could guess, he announced Gwenyth was no longer in the picture. "She waited until I left for work to pack up and leave without a trace."

Diana could have made fun of him, but she did the opposite. She laid her hands over his and held them tightly. She actually felt bad for him. She saw how madly in love they were . . . until she broke Gwen's nose, that is. Unlike Tom, Diana was sympathetic.

She looked deep into his eyes. "Tom, I'm really sorry."

One side of his mouth curved up. "Are you really?" he asked with a hint of sarcasm.

She almost laughed. "I mean . . . I'm really sorry for breaking her nose."

They both chuckled. She was happy he could find some humor in his misery.

"No, the baseball tryouts were just one issue of many. We had been fighting before that," he explained. "Gwenyth lost her job a week earlier due to costing the company ninety grand. And if you can believe it, she was upset with me because I told her that it was her own fault. The cherry on top was her accusing me of siding with you about her nose."

"I swear I didn't mean for that to happen!"

Tom laughed. "I know. We also read Jordan's injury waiver. It was flawless."

"I don't know what to tell you about her getting fired," Diana said. *Other than she had it coming.* "Ninety grand is a lot of money, though. How is the studying going?"

"I took a few practice tests and have done exceptionally well. Johnson, Larkens, and Lewis wants to hold a spot for me at their firm. That is, when I pass."

"Oh wow," she said with a smile. "That's where you're doing your internship, right? That's only seven miles from your place."

He rose from his seat and pulled her in for a deep embrace. She could feel his heart pounding against her cheek. Her eyes softened. *I miss his smell—citrus cookies.*

"It can be your place, too."

Diana took a step back and looked down at her feet. She refused to let go of all the things he did to her. "Tom . . . we can't."

He stepped closer to her, his hands touching her elbows. He leaned his head forward and closed his eyes, but she pulled away before he could kiss her. She needed and deserved an explanation.

"All right," he said as his eyes veered to the floor, "we need to talk about this."

She held her breath for a few seconds and then deeply exhaled. She was nervous beyond belief. This was the moment she had been waiting for. It was long overdue.

"Okay," she murmured. "Go on."

"We'll both need to sit for this." He motioned for her to sit beside him. As soon as she did, he slowly exhaled and lowered his gaze. He seemed ashamed. "First, I want to say how terribly sorry I am for cheating and making your life a living hell. You didn't deserve any of that."

Diana bit her lip, then began massaging the base of her left thumb with her other hand. "How did you meet?"

"It was a little over a year ago while I was bartending at my other job. At first, it was just an innocent flirtation."

Diana's eyes widened as he elaborated. "I swear I didn't mean anything by it. I overheard her phone conversation with a friend. She was having a bad day. A coworker of hers was constantly reporting on her at work, so I gave her a free shot of whiskey."

Diana was laughing on the inside. *So, it was me who started this mess?*

Tom rubbed his brows with his thumb and index finger. "I just wanted to make her day, you know? We talked that entire night until the bar closed. I thought our friendship was simply platonic until she stopped by that next evening."

Diana nodded as her brows furrowed. "So that's when—"

"No. Actually, I told her that I had a girlfriend, but she didn't seem to care. She just kept showing up every night."

"For how long?"

"For about a month." Tom's voice quivered. "And that's when . . . I lost control."

Diana remained silent to absorb his words.

"After the affair started, I felt so confused about our relationship. It was like I forgot who I was. A part of me wanted to make things right with you, but at the same time, I couldn't get Gwenyth out of my mind." Tom tried holding back his tears. "I resorted to drinking my problems away. I became an alcoholic."

Diana gasped as her hand covered her mouth.

"And that's why I became angrier with myself, with you, and everyone else. I tried coming up with excuses to justify my infidelity. I even tried stirring arguments so you could leave me, but you chose to stay."

Diana shook her head as she pressed her palms over her eyes. His words were hard to digest.

"I feel so terrible for causing you pain. I should have been honest with you from the start. Instead, I made matters worse. Our home became a second hell for you, and it was my fault. Diana, I'm so sorry."

"Are you okay now?" she asked, sobbing. "I mean . . . with the drinking?"

He tilted his head to meet her gaze. "I've gotten better, if that's what you're asking. I've been attending meetings."

Diana nodded again as she wiped her nose. She felt Tom's hand on her cheek as he spoke softly. "I know this is painful for you to hear, but it's really helping me."

They both looked at each other for a second and lost it. She didn't mean to laugh. Diana's eyes veered to the table where she argued with her mother. She had an important question to ask.

"I need to know something. . . Did I contribute to your affair in any way?"

He paused. He looked away for a brief moment, then sighed. His expression clearly answered her question.

"How, Tom?" she sobbed. "What did I do?"

He grabbed her hands and kissed them. "I need you listen to me without interrupting because what I have to tell you is very important and serious."

"Okay."

"Diana, do you remember that when we first moved out here, I told you that you could start fresh? That you could be anyone and do anything without your parents controlling you?"

"Yes."

"I thought things were going to get better. I thought that you were going to be more confident in yourself and be more adventurous, but it was like you were too comfortable in your own cage. Every time I tried to get you out, you refused my help, and you would constantly talk down on yourself. Over the years, I grew more impatient and frustrated with you. There were times when I felt so useless to you, like whatever I did for you wasn't good enough."

She put her hands together and pressed them against her nose and mouth. She tightly shut her eyes, painfully accepting his reasoning. *He's right. He's so right.*

"The way that you carried yourself . . . it just became very unattractive to me. Every time you wanted to make love, I felt disgusted with myself because I knew that I was making love to a broken woman. At the same time, it felt like you wanted me to treat you that way, so I did."

Tom's eyes became glossy again. Diana couldn't hold herself back anymore. She had never seen this sensitive side of him. Emotionally, he was beaten down. She hugged him and didn't want to let him go.

"I'm so sorry."

He wrapped his arms around her and rested his chin over her head. "It's okay," he whispered.

She shook her head against his chest. "It's not. I can't believe that I made you feel that way."

She felt his warm lips press against the top of her head. "You've changed. I can see that now."

She knew what he was waiting for. As soon as she lifted her head, he kissed her passionately. Her heart skipped a beat. She melted right into him as she kissed him back. *Oh Tom, I want to so badly. But this also feels wrong. This can't be happening!*

She broke their kiss with a small push. He leaned in for another, but she turned her head away, leaving him to kiss her cheek.

She covered her mouth with the back of her hand. "I'm sorry. We shouldn't."

"Diana, what can I do to make things right with you? Please give me another chance."

She remembered what happened when she asked him that very same question and almost stumbled over her words. "I'm, I'm afraid that you'll . . . lose control of your anger with me again. We had moments when—"

"I know how you feel about my temper. I just want you to know that I am getting help."

She wiped her tears with her hands. "You mean it?"

He nodded. "If you want, you can go to counseling with me. We can even go back to church."

"You're willing to do that?"

"Yes, I'll do whatever it takes. Diana, I can be many things, but I am not, and I will never be, Charles Quinn. I hope you know that. I will never beat you. You have my solemn word that I will never hurt you again."

She began to smile.

He reached for his pocket and knelt forward, revealing what appeared to be an engagement box. *What? Oh my God!* She hunched over toward him and waved her hands.

"Tom—"

"Diana, please let me have my moment. I want to declare my love for you and officially solidify our relationship."

Her eyes widened when he opened the box before her. It was a three-stone ring that boasted round diamonds and a radiant cut ruby center. Although it was beautiful, it was different than what she imagined. Red was not Diana's favorite color, but asking him why he chose that ring would have ruined everything.

"I had this in our closet for a while. I kept waiting for the right opportunity to ask, but never got the chance."

Diana covered her smile with her hand, "It's . . . so beautiful."

He slid the ring on her finger. "Then say yes and be mine forever."

Diana wanted to say yes. Her heart ached for her to say it, but her mind was telling her to say the opposite. *I need to think this over very carefully.* Tom waited for her answer.

"Diana."

She was nervous, but needed to be honest. "I . . . umm, I need a little time to think about it."

He grunted as he picked himself up off the floor. "I need you to give me a straight answer."

"Why the rush?"

"Well, I suppose I can wait. It's just that we've been together for eight years and I really don't want to wait anymore."

"I see."

"I'm going to get the career of my dreams and I know that I will finally be able to support you." He put his arm around her again and smiled. "I don't care if you get this job or any other job. I'll be fine with you being my housewife . . . and hopefully a stay-at-home mother shortly after."

Diana blushed.

His smile widened. "I'll take care of you from now on."

Suddenly, she felt the winds calling from her bedroom. The book was ready to stir another cyclone. *Fuck! Not now!* She needed to get Tom out of the house quickly.

"I love you. I want to say yes, but please give me a little time."

He held her up by her waist and pressed his lips against hers. Diana's hands landed on his shoulders, and she gently pushed herself off.

Tom smiled. "When will you give me an answer?"

She had to think fast. "How about Saturday?"

"This Saturday? Sure. Okay."

"Umm, Tom?"

"Hmm?"

She spoke fast as she rushed him to the door. "I need you to go now. I forgot that I needed to do something. It's kind of an emergency, and I don't have time to explain."

"What?"

"Please!" She pulled on the knob.

"Wait!" he demanded.

Before she closed the door on him, he snuck another kiss.

"Saturday," he confirmed. "Meet me at the Lunar Café by our apartment! I'll text you on the time."

"Okay!"

He smiled. "I love you!"

"I love you too!"

Diana shut the door, locked it, and ran to her room. She had no time to admire the engagement ring on her finger. She opened the book to Chapter 19. *Geez! Hold your horses! I swear I'm going to give that Narrator a piece of my mind! What a weird Christmas this is!*

Chapter 17

Diana found herself in a dim room lit only by candlelight. Although it was mostly dark, she could see everything. Limestone served as the inner curtain of her room. It was the same stone that was plastered beneath her feet. The flooring was not level, so it threw off her balance. The space was more of a rotunda with a wooden canopy bed draped in silk blue curtains. She had found herself in the garret of a tower, where she enjoyed a full view of the starlit sky, the ocean from afar, and the comforting darkness that could almost make anyone drift to sleep. It was a beautiful, peaceful night.

Unfortunately, she couldn't enjoy it. She was too annoyed by the book's demanding summons and of course, it didn't allow her to read the beginning of the chapter. As soon as she opened it, she was immediately sucked in. She did accept some fault in the matter. She could have read the chapter yesterday, but she let her emotions get the best of her. *Today would have been my day off.* She was also upset about forcing Tom out of the house. She couldn't enjoy their moment of love and forgiveness.

She quickly looked at herself to determine what era this chapter took place in. She wore a dark violet gown with a laced black bodice that enhanced her womanly figure. Underneath was a low-cut, silky white camise. This time, though, she had long auburn hair. With her hand, she pinched a lock of it and waved it in front of her face. She grimaced as it was the same shade as Gwenyth's.

"Welcome back, Diana!" The Narrator cheered with delight. "I see that you didn't have time to—Oh my God What is *that*?"

His spastic voice made her jump and scream. Diana looked around, but she didn't see anything to fuss over. She started to panic.

"What? What is what?" she screeched.

The Narrator gasped with exaggeration. "That . . . thing on your hand."

Diana looked at her hand and realized her engagement ring had not disappeared like the rest of her normal clothing. She rolled her eyes.

"Okay! First of all, don't scare me like that again! I thought there was a troll or a bug in the room! Second, this is called a ring." Diana waved her ring finger in the air. "Though I don't know how it made its way here."

The Narrator laughed. "But it's on your left hand. Who claimed you?"

Diana bit her lower lip before answering. "Tom."

"*The* Tom?" he scoffed.

Diana nodded with slight embarrassment.

"The cheating scumbag loser who throws tantrums? The so-called 'man' who blames you for bad sex, but who can't even give you an orgasm? That Tom?"

Diana felt the heat rush into her cheeks. "We made up! Also, not everything has to be about sex! It's not that important, and I've had enough good sex here to last me a lifetime!"

The Narrator couldn't control his laughter. "I don't believe you."

"I mean . . . okay. Yes, I have enjoyed my time here and all. But it's not real! None of this is real!"

She could hear the disappointment in his voice. "It's more real here than that gem you're wearing."

"What do you mean? Are you saying it's fake?"

"Sadly, I know you better than your fiancé does," he argued. "You don't even like red!"

Diana lifted her hand in front of her face and started intently. "It looks real to me, and I can get used to the color!"

"I meant the love, you clueless doormat!" he yelled. "All the men that you have laid with were truly in love with you! Even that pesky Sir Fucksalot who you convinced to dip his churro into the king's chocolate!"

Diana's face turned red. "Hey! He ended up liking it!"

The Narrator laughed. "These men will do *anything* for you, and you play with them like they're toys."

"Hold on!" Diana yelled. "Why do you care all of a sudden? And how exactly do you know me better? You're just a silly narrator!"

"You're right, Diana," his voice lowered. "I'm just a narrator, but do me a favor and define what that is for a second."

Diana paused to think, but couldn't come up with anything clever to say.

"That's what I thought!" He chuckled. "I tell it like it is."

"Okay, Mr. Know-it-all," she argued, "besides my carnal desires being fulfilled, what else am I supposed to get out of all this?"

WOOSH! CRASH! BOOM! Loud explosions coming from all directions interrupted them. She ran to the window and saw hundreds of fiery arrows piercing the night sky. Two opposing forces were deep in battle. The one shooting arrows had an army of knights wearing white and blue cloaks. The other army stood guard in front of her tower and wore black garments with dark armor. They yelled as they raced down the hill with their swords and spears.

Catapults unleashed firebombs in her direction as she took cover beneath the window. They missed the tower by a few inches. She peeked out to get a better look.

One knight in a blue cloak removed his crowned helmet and recognized her immediately. He had a long blond beard that was neatly combed and braided. He stared at her with his piercing blue eyes. Although handsome, he had an intimidating expression. "Princess Tamara is in the tower!" he shouted to his men. "Cease fire!"

Diana felt her room shake. Something was definitely adding pressure onto the spire above her. The stone ceiling was cracking, sending dust down over her head. From the window, she looked up to find a huge black dragon, as big as a dragon could ever be! Its loud roar made Diana scream and cower back inside. The tower shook as it jumped off. She took shelter by the bed, panicked. Through the window, she could see fire blasting through the sky and men screaming in agony. There was no escape from this fiery hell. Diana ran to the door, but she was locked in. She rolled her eyes. *Really?*

She yelled at The Narrator. "Gee, a princess locked up in a tower guarded by a fiery evil dragon? How original!"

He responded with his usual, sarcastic tone. "Well, it seems you have it all figured out."

There was nothing Diana could do. She flung herself onto the bed.

"I guess I'll wait for my rescuer."

"I can't wait to see how this ends."

She lifted her head slightly. "What do you mean?"

A grappling hook made its way over the stone base of the tower window. Someone was climbing up. Diana blushed while anticipating quality time with her rescuer. *The sooner this is over, the better.* When she heard his armored body clank against the floor, she rose from the bed and smiled. She taunted him as she played with her auburn hair.

It was the same man who recognized her from the battlefield. He gave her that same look.

Diana laid back down with her arms behind her head. She waited comfortably for him to join her . . . until she heard him draw out his long sword. She searched for any possible foe in the room, but it was just the two of them. He charged at her, but she rolled off the bed and landed on the stone floor. She winced as she held her knee to her chest. Before she knew it, the man jumped over the bed. His sword pointed down, aiming for her back. Just in the nick of time, she rolled under the bed and dodged his blow. His sword hit the floor, causing the stone to fracture beneath him. She heard him grunt in frustration as he tried lifting the frame, but it was too heavy.

"What the *fuck* is going on?" Diana yelled out.

The Narrator laughed.

"This isn't funny!" she screeched.

With some determination, the knight finally flipped the bed over. He laughed as he picked up his sword again. Diana got up on her feet and waved her hands in front of him.

"Stop! Stop!"

Surprisingly, the man paused and waited for her to speak.

She cleared her throat. "I'm sure whatever is going on, we can work out some kind of a truce."

The Narrator intervened. "Diana, this is Prince Lucien, your betrothed. He joined forces with your father, King Barath, to slay the dragon and kill you."

Diana gulped. "Why?"

Prince Lucien then spoke. "*Why?* Why did you betray your kind and bed this monster?"

"What monster?" she asked.

"The dragon!"

Diana paused for a moment and squinted her eyes. "How is that even physically possible?"

The prince gripped his sword, ready to charge again. He smiled smugly as he pointed it toward her. She found herself pinned against the wall. There was no escape. All the things that she had endured flashed before her eyes. Emotionally, she was still in pain. With tears in her eyes, she cried to The Narrator.

"Okay, I'm sorry! You win! You were right about me this whole time!"

"Diana, I have no control over this!" he urged. "You need to fight him!"

Instead, she fell to her knees and bawled hysterically. She wanted to give up. Prince Lucien just stood there, entertained. Diana began counting with her fingers, listing all her issues.

"I lost my only friend. She doesn't even want to talk to me anymore. My mom doesn't think I deserve better. Who knows? Maybe she's right. My father is a real asshole. It's no wonder I have all these issues, and you are right about Tom. I can't . . ."

She shook her head.

"Diana, please don't cry," The Narrator replied.

"I *am* a clueless doormat," she sobbed. "My life is falling apart, and nothing I do is ever good enough!"

"You make me laugh. No other host has done that for me. No other host has cared about me."

Diana and The Narrator were interrupted by Prince Lucien. Her self-loathing and tears made him drop his sword and laugh uncontrollably. If he wasn't wearing a codpiece, Diana would have kicked him where he deserved.

The Narrator sounded surprised. "Okay, I've never seen him react this way. Ever."

"Seeing you begging for your life. . ." Prince Lucien laughed in between his words. "Hearing all your sorrows gives me great pleasure."

Diana clenched her jaw and stared with disgust. "Eww."

"Well, that's not creepy," The Narrator murmured sarcastically.

Lucien's laughing came to an end when the door burst open. A tall man with a dark hooded cape walked in. "It's you!" The prince spat as he picked up his sword again.

The man stepped in front of Diana and helped her off the floor. He removed his hood and revealed himself to her. He had short, ashy brown hair. His squared jawline and prominent chin looked like they were sculpted by angels. She stared deeply into his enticing amber eyes, which reminded her of fall leaves infiltrated by sunlight. He smiled as he touched her cheek, but then he noticed her tears. His brows narrowed as he whispered in her ear.

"He will rue the day he caused you pain."

"Huh?" Diana uttered.

"That's the dragon," The Narrator explained. "Tion, your lover."

"Ohh!" She blushed. *Okay, he must have transformed because that would be the only way.*

He turned to face the prince, who was already backing up toward the window. There was no escape. Tion's eyes deepened before he exhaled a blaze of raging fire from his mouth. The intense flames danced over the prince and melted his armor. He screamed in anguish as he stumbled out the window. Before his body hit the ground, he was completely incinerated.

Diana was stunned. *Well, that was easy. He got rid of him with one blow—literally.*

Tion moved closer to her. Before she could say anything, he held her close and wrapped his strong arms around her.

"Princess," he murmured. "I apologize for the delay."

"That's all right." Diana blushed.

He kissed her softly against her cheek. "Are you hurt, my love?"

"No." She lifted her head to meet his gaze and wrapped her arms around his neck.

"You have my condolences. Your father wouldn't yield. He met his demise quickly."

For whatever reason, Diana felt a sense of relief. She didn't know who this King Barath was, nor did she care. There was just something about Tion's face and the way he held her that made her feel safe. Perhaps it was because she secretly wished that he was referring to Charles. *If only you truly existed in my life.* Her hand reached up to caress his face. He grabbed it with his own and rubbed his cheek against the inside her palm.

"I'm sorry, my love. I had to."

"Thank you for rescuing me," she smiled. "Thank you for protecting me."

She pressed her soft lips against his, which fed a flame of passion between them. His hands roamed along her backside, gripping onto her curves. Her arm hung around his shoulder as she let her other hand slide down. He gasped with pleasure before he pressed her gently against the stone wall. One hand held the back of her head as his tongue pressed between her parted lips. He grinned before he turned her over and lifted her dress.

It was an unforgettable night of pleasure. Without a care in the world, they let the land burn along with their enemies. Now that the evil king and prince were dead, there was nobody left to challenge Tion's reign. The war was over, and a new kingdom would rise from the ashes.

Chapter 18

B y the time she made it back to her world, it was already eight in the morning. Apparently, the dragon chapter took longer than expected. It was no surprise that she wasn't tired. Every time a chapter was exceptionally good, she would feel a huge rush of adrenaline flowing through her veins. Today, she felt as if she could effortlessly conquer a triathlon. The lovemaking was merely a fraction of the immense joy she felt. Riding Tion in his dragon form was an exhilarating and enchanting experience. She felt as though she were a true dragon princess, gracefully soaring through the night sky.

Even though Diana had a wonderful time, she was still beside herself with all these unanswered questions. She paced around her room. *How many chapters do I have left? Is there something else that I need to get out of this? I can't be doing this forever, especially if I decide to marry Tom.*

"Tom! Oh crap!"

Diana snatched up her phone, finding two missed calls and five text messages from him last night. She scrolled through them and gulped with fear. Each message was almost two hours apart. The last one was sent at three o'clock.

> **Tom:** *I'm so glad that we were able to forgive each other.*

> **Tom:** *I love you.*

> **Tom:** *I can't wait to marry you. That is, if you say yes.*

> **Tom:** *I know it's late, but how busy are you? Can you please call me back?*

> **Tom:** *Are you okay? Call me back.*

She slapped her forehead with the palm of her hand. She felt her stomach twisting into knots. She had to respond, but she felt a sudden reluctance. Yesterday, they managed to forgive each other, but she wasn't given much time to absorb their moment. She didn't want to lie to him or put on some façade to accommodate his feelings while she sorted out her own.

The truth was difficult for her to accept. If Lena hadn't shown up, she wouldn't have fought with Jordan. If she wasn't in a vulnerable state, she probably would have acted differently with Tom. Her mind was telling her what she already knew. She'd be a fool if she said yes to his proposal. Her heart, on the other hand, was forgiving and held all the precious memories of him. *Tom was not always horrible. Like he said, he strayed when he didn't know how else to help me. People make mistakes, and nobody is perfect. My mom was right; this was my fault too.*

Diana also considered her recent disagreement with The Narrator. Although it was painful to hear, he reminded her of what her long-term relationship lacked. Sex was important, especially the intimacy and passion. Every lover that she took on was more experienced. Sure, Diana learned a few cool tricks to spice things up in the bedroom, but was Tom willing to please her as much as what she had become accustomed to? It was impossible to imagine Tom ever measuring up. *Yes, sex is important, but doesn't love conquer all obstacles?* She looked at the ring once more and sighed. *I don't know what to do.*

Diana knew there was no easy answer. She tossed her phone in the air and then caught it with both hands. *At the very least, I need to call Tom and apologize for not answering sooner.* She gave it one more toss. As it made its way down, her phone rang. The noise startled her, but she managed to catch it. Her thumb accidentally hit the Answer button, but it wasn't a number she recognized. *Crap*!

She gritted her teeth before placing the phone to her ear. "Hello?"

"Hi. Is this Miss Diana Quinn?" His voice sounded familiar, but she couldn't make out who it was.

She responded with a friendlier tone. "This is she!"

"Hi, Diana. I'm so glad you answered. This is Jerry Wilcox."

Diana's heart pounded. "Hi, Mr. Wilcox! It's a pleasure hearing from you. I hope you had a wonderful Christmas."

"I did," he said warmly. "I hope the same for you."

"Absolutely." She nervously giggled.

"Well, the reason why I'm calling you is because I looked further into your background and viewed samples of your work from that internship. I have to say . . . I'm very impressed."

"Oh!" Her eyes widened.

"You are overqualified to be an assistant. How would you feel if I offered you an editor's position? It just opened up."

Diana was stunned. "Wow, umm . . . wow."

Jerry laughed. "I'm giving you a chance because I know you have what it takes. I also like you. Just say yes."

His laugh brought her joy. Diana almost burst into tears. "Yes! Mr. Wilcox, thank you so much for this amazing opportunity!"

"You're all right, kid. Orientation starts tomorrow at eleven. Don't be late."

Diana jumped up and down with glee. *Oh my God! I can't wait to tell Tom!* She immediately went to her contacts screen and dialed his number. Her body still shook with excitement.

He answered immediately. "Diana?"

"Tom, I—"

"I've been waiting for your call." His voice grew angrier. "I was so worried that I almost drove back to make sure you were okay!"

"I'm so sorry. I didn't mean to wor—"

"I mean, you couldn't at least text me back?"

Diana felt her heart sink. "Tom, I'm really sorry. There was just so much going on . . . and I have some news."

"Yeah, what?"

She hesitated at first. She knew her words weren't going to make a difference. "I just got hired as an editor."

"Oh."

Diana bit her bottom lip. *Not even a congratulations?*

He continued. "Well, good for you, I guess. That still doesn't explain why you couldn't pick up the phone."

She spoke sincerely. "Tom, I'm really sorry."

"You know, you rushed me out of the house without giving me a straight answer. That really wasn't fair to me. I need to see you so we can get to the bottom of this."

Her free hand massaged her temples. "Right, I know."

He sighed in frustration. "Can we meet today instead of Saturday? I feel like I need to resolve this issue we have."

"Issue?"

"Yes." He lowered his tone. "I know that you have some concerns about our relationship, and I want to put your mind at ease."

"Tom, of course I want to see you, but today isn't good. I have orientation tomorrow, and it might last the whole day."

"Okay, I guess I need to wait then. What's another two days, really?"

Diana didn't know how else to respond. To diffuse the situation, she answered the only way she knew how. As much as she hated it, she gave him what he was expecting. After all, he was "right," and she was "wrong." She softened her voice, which instantly admitted defeat.

"You are right. I don't have a good explanation as to why I wasn't responsive. I didn't consider your feelings and I'm truly sorry. I hope you can forgive me."

He paused before responding. "Are you still wearing the ring?"

She didn't lie. "Yes. I haven't taken it off, if that's what you're wondering."

"Good. I love you."

A crushing weight settled over her chest. "I love you too. I'm sorry I worried you."

"It's fine. Meet me at the Lunar Café on Saturday. Let's shoot for nine o'clock."

"Okay then."

He disconnected the call. She could tell that he was still pissed off. It was understandable, but how many times must she apologize for him to get over it? Yes, she rushed him out of the house. Yes, she didn't give him a clear answer on his proposal. She told him that she was busy and that she had an emergency.

Maybe that's why he was so worried. Maybe he thought it was serious.

In the end, he made it all about his feelings—talk about gaslighting. Of course, Diana avoided that perception by slipping back to her old, less confident self. What was she going to do about it, though? For now, she took off the ring and left it on her nightstand. *I can't even right now.*

The loud, high-pitched grinding of the garage door startled her. Diana's head perked up. *Could it be?* She ran out of her bedroom toward the kitchen and faced the laundry room door. She gasped as it opened. As soon as their glazed eyes met, they ran toward each other for the biggest embrace.

"Jordan, oh my God!" Diana wiped the tears from her friend's cheeks. "I'm so sorry."

"No, I should be the one apologizing to you. I'm really sorry for the way I have behaved. I didn't mean to make you feel worse."

Diana started to cry. "It's not your fault. You were only trying to protect me."

"I need to talk to you. I need to tell you everything," Jordan sniffled. "I've been the worst friend to you, and I don't know if you'll ever forgive me or still want to be friends."

Diana couldn't believe what she was hearing. "How have you been the worst friend? You've been nothing but nice to me. I feel like I've been the one taking advantage of you. I couldn't even buy you a Christmas present."

She shook her head. "You know that stuff never bothers me, right?"

Diana gave her another hug. "I need to tell you something too, but I'm also afraid of losing you as a friend."

She gave her a small chuckle. "So, we've both been bad, huh?"

"Well, I've never seen you this upset before . . . so, this must be very serious."

They walked to the kitchen table and sat across from each other.

"I'm really sorry about how I've behaved. There is no excuse. It's just that when I heard what happened to you. I just lost it." Jordan grabbed a napkin and wiped her nose. "All I can really say is that I know how you feel because . . ."

She took a deep breath as she looked down at her lap, then met Diana's gaze again. "When I was a kid, I grew up in 'the system' and lived with several Lenas and Charleses."

Diana reached over to hold Jordan's hand. She could feel it shaking beneath hers as Jordan continued. "And I understand why you didn't want to tell me because I never wanted to tell anyone about my past."

"Jordan, I'm so sorry."

She nodded with her eyes closed.

"How?" Diana paused to clear her throat. "How did you get through it?"

"How, huh? I still struggle. I struggle every day. Everyone automatically assumes that I'm strong on the inside as well as the outside just by looking at me. The truth is I work out a lot for my mental and emotional health. It's what motivates me to be successful and happy every single day. It's exactly how writing helps you. I really hope you don't ever give that up. Every time you write, I notice a significant change within you."

Diana cracked a small smile. "That's why you gifted me the laptop?"

"Yeah."

"I hope you know that you can always be vulnerable with me. I won't ever make fun of you. Your secrets are always safe with me."

"Thank you. I really appreciate it. I didn't mean to scare you either. I just lost it with your mom. I wanted to smack her so hard."

Diana's smile widened. "Was that all you wanted to tell me?"

"No." She shook her head as she folded her lips in.

"Well?"

"There's a lot more than you think," she muttered. "I lied to you... a few times."

"About what?"

"Okay!" Jordan slammed her hand against the table and then held it with agony as she spoke quickly. "I helped you get the job interview! Sherry is my boss, and she knows Jerry Wilcox."

Diana let out an exaggerated gasp. "Jordan!"

"I know!" She groaned as her hand landed over her face, covering her eyes.

Diana laughed. "Figures."

"What?" Jordan peeked in between her fingers.

"Come on, Jordan. I sort of knew you were up to something when I asked you who she was. You immediately changed the subject."

Jordan nearly fell off her chair as she exhaled with relief.

"I wanted to say thank you. And just so you know, I got the job."

She jumped from her seat. "For real? The assistant position?"

Diana shook her head and grinned. "An editor's position!"

They leapt to their feet and shrieked with joy. "You're amazing!" Jordan cheered. "I knew you could do it!"

"Okay, is there anything else you would like to share?"

Terror shrouded Jordan's face. This was it, the big enchilada of all secrets. Jordan nodded, but she seemed to have trouble making eye contact. "Well, the man that I've been seeing—"

"Your secret lover?"

"I've known him for quite some time. At first, I thought it wasn't going to be anything, but then one thing led to another. And for a while, I wasn't comfortable telling you or anyone about it and—"

"Well, that's understandable," Diana interrupted. "I mean with work and publicity—you said it yourself—it had to be confidential."

"For a while, it was."

"Was?" Diana's eyes widened.

"It was okay for us to disclose our relationship months ago, but I decided not to. There were times when I really wanted to tell you about him, but then you would get into the worst fights with Tom. I just felt like the timing was always off."

Diana felt horrible. "I'm sorry, Jordan. I put you through so much with my drama, especially during the past couple of weeks. It has been always about me. I feel like I've been such a bad friend."

Jordan shook her head. "Not 'always,' and you're not a bad friend!"

"Really?"

"As a matter of fact, you have helped me become a more compassionate and sensitive person. You're like the little sister that I never had and who I always want to protect."

Diana smiled with happy tears. "So . . . are you going to tell me who this man is?"

Jordan took a deep breath and nodded, "It's Leif—"

"Oh my God!" Diana gasped. "Leif Hendricks?"

Jordan bit her bottom lip and slowly nodded.

"Ahh!"

Jordan plugged her ears with her fingers and laughed. In all the Texas games they saw together on TV and on the field, he was always there. It was Leif The Lion. Leif The Legend.

"How long? How long have you been seeing him?"

"About a year," she giggled. "But we made it official seven months ago."

"Wow! Wait? Is that where you went for Christmas? Did you go to Texas?"

Jordan nodded. "Yes, he got me a late flight and I met his family."

"You know what's coming next, don't you?" They giggled as Diana rubbed her hands together. "I'm so happy for you."

"So, you're not mad?"

"Of course not. I want nothing but the best for you, as always, and I want you to know that I always look up to you as my big sister." Her head dropped to her hands as she began to sob. "You always look after me, and I appreciate all that you've done, but I don't want you to worry about me anymore."

Jordan moved closer to her. "What's wrong?"

Diana tried to joke at first. "Are you done with your confessions?"

She nodded and gave her a half-smile. "Yours can't possibly be as bad as mine."

"I don't want us to fight anymore. I want us to always be friends. Even if . . ."

She couldn't seem to finish her sentence. She knew Jordan was going to be disappointed.

"Even if what?"

"Even if I decide to get back with Tom."

Jordan crossed her arms and leaned back against her chair. She closed her eyes for a few seconds and then looked at her again. She spoke calmly, which Diana appreciated. "Go on."

"After you left, I was very depressed and felt so unguarded. I don't know why, but he showed up, as if he already knew. Please don't be mad."

"So, he's no longer with Gwen?"

Diana shook her head as she held her breath in.

"I see," Jordan murmured. "So, you forgave each other?"

"Yes," Diana said quietly, "but I feel so confused and stuck."

She didn't want to tell Jordan about Tom's proposal, especially when she was trying to keep an open mind.

"You see," Diana nervously twiddled her thumbs, "Tom was not always horrible. You know that I met him in high school and everything, but what you don't know is that he was always there to protect me from my dad. He used to be so good to me."

Jordan nodded.

"Things changed after we moved here. I always had a problem with self-confidence and you, of all people, know that I still struggle with it."

Jordan looked straight into her eyes. "You have gotten better. I especially noticed it during tryouts. You were doing so great without him. Diana, please don't take him back."

Diana sniffled. "You need to understand that I'm not perfect and that I did play a part in his affair, and—"

Jordan shook her head. "Please, you need to hear me out. You did not play a part in his cheating. If he was a real man, he would have confronted you with his issues and he would have at least ended things respectfully."

"Yeah, but—"

"You have a heart of gold for forgiving him, I give you that. Why can't you just express your gratitude for what he did for you and move on? You can both be apart and still grow."

She sighed. "Jordan, we've been together for eight years. Do you know how hard that is to do?"

"I understand, but people change. Tom is not the man he was eight years ago. He's not even the man he was two years ago. What makes you think he's the man that you deserve now?"

Diana didn't know how to respond. It was a valid question.

Jordan held her hands together and pressed them under her chin. "He's treated you so poorly. I hope you don't believe that you deserve that."

Diana looked away and nodded.

"You actually do?"

She nodded again as her eyes veered to the floor.

"No! You should never, ever settle for that garbage. You should never allow anyone to disrespect you, to abuse you."

"He never intentionally laid a hand on me." Diana's eyes returned. "Yes, he said some hurtful things, but he never struck me."

Jordan tucked a strand of hair behind Diana's ear. Her lips pursed with rage. "Don't kid yourself. Your bruises were no accident."

Diana's eyes widened as Jordan continued. "You didn't think I noticed? How do you think physical abuse starts? I saw this over and over in my childhood. On top of that, I've witnessed him hurt you verbally and emotionally. For now, he's probably showing you his good side. I'm afraid that you'll walk in your mom's footsteps: Married to scum, jobless, and with no way out. If you have children with him, are you going to allow him to hurt them the way he hurts you?"

The words stung. Diana had always envisioned herself marrying Tom, but never thought that she could end up like her mother. She remembered what Tom said before he left the house, that she could be his stay-at-home wife and mother shortly after. *Oh God, Jordan is right. If I have children with him . . . No, I need to talk to him. I need to know for sure that he wouldn't . . .*

"You know that I will do anything for you. You are my best friend, my sister—I will support you no matter what—but if you take him back, I will no longer get involved."

Diana nodded. "I love you, Jordan. I understand, and I don't want you to get involved. I just need time to think things over. Let's not fight anymore, okay?"

Jordan smiled back and gave her another hug. Diana knew she was disappointed in her and knew she had every right to be. Getting back with Tom would be like jumping back into the lion's den. In her heart, she knew she would be putting herself at risk if she were to accept his proposal, but their history and all the good moments they had together left her torn.

A loud bark that sounded like it was coming from outside interrupted them. Diana looked around the room and noticed Bandit wasn't with them.

"Jordan! You didn't leave Bandit outside, did you?"

She grinned. "About that . . . there's somebody I want you to meet."

"What?!" Diana panicked. She could feel her heart racing. "Is Leif—"

Jordan chuckled as she waltzed to the front door.

"No, wait! My face!"

"Your face is fine!" she argued playfully.

They both heard him from the other side of the door. "If it's any consolation, I'm the ugliest crier in the world."

Diana's cheeks flushed. *Was he listening to us the entire time?*

Jordan giggled as she opened the door. Diana was almost blinded by the ray of light that entered the foyer. She recognized the tall, manly figure from his games. His long, coppery hair was tied back. His radiant smile made her heart leap out of her chest. He had one arm looped around Bandit and with his other, he held a large bouquet of pink roses. Jordan smiled as he leaned over to kiss her. His voice made Diana giddy.

"Did you miss me?"

Jordan laughed as she took off his blue aviators, revealing his warm brown eyes. "You were gone for a while."

He set Bandit on the floor before giving her another kiss. Jordan's eyes then directed him to look over his shoulder. He smiled as he turned to Diana. Then he walked towards her, holding the bouquet.

"You must be Diana."

She remained motionless. If she tried to say anything, she would fail miserably.

He moved closer to her, leaving hardly any space between them. She felt the flowers graze her shirt.

He smiled once more as he gently pushed them toward her. "These are for you."

Diana was taken by surprise, but didn't mean to make it so obvious. He laughed as he took her arms and wrapped them around her bouquet.

"I hope you like them."

She looked down to admire them, hiding her teary eyes in the process. She didn't remember the last time anyone had given her flowers. She gasped as she felt Leif pull her in for a hug as if they were already close friends.

"I know that it's been rough."

Diana closed her eyes and smiled naturally. "Thank you."

When she could open her eyes without spilling any tears over his arm, she saw Jordan smiling from the corner. Diana knew Leif was perfect for her friend in every way, and she was ecstatic to see where their relationship went. It only took a few moments for her to get used to his celebrity status. They spent the rest of the day getting to know each other while eating Chinese takeout and playing Monopoly.

"You know," Leif smirked as he rolled the dice, "if you decide to ditch him, I can introduce you to a few players who are looking for wives."

Diana's face turned red. "Umm."

Jordan laughed. "That doesn't sound like a bad idea, actually."

Later that evening, Jordan took Leif out for a night out on the town. They invited Diana to join them, but she kindly declined. She wanted them to have a moment alone and knew that she would only be a third wheel.

It was impossible for her to deny that her heart ached to be loved in the same way. Diana went back to her bedroom for some soul-searching. She glanced at the ring Tom gave her and sighed miserably.

She threw herself onto the bed and checked her phone. *No messages from him. He is probably still upset with me, and there's nothing that I can do about it.*

Diana remembered everything that Jordan said to her. Deep down, she knew her friend was right about him. *What makes me think that he's the best I deserve? I don't know. I guess I'm just an outcast. I can only take what I can get and make do with it. If I'm ever lucky enough to find love—true love—that's even real, clearly, I wouldn't be worthy of it. I don't deserve it.*

A familiar yet intrusive voice crept its way into her head at that moment: "*Deserve nothing.*" She tossed and turned as her traumatizing past invaded. She remembered every word her father spat into her ears after he dragged her by her hair across their living room floor. Between every punch, he yelled out words that broke her spirit.

"You little bitch!"

"You deserve nothing!"

"Call the police now! I wish you would! Let's see what happens!"

"This is for trying to embarrass your mother!"

"And this one . . . this is for me!"

His final punch left her bleeding on the tile floor and urinating on herself out of fear. He laughed sadistically at her humiliation. She scrunched on her side, trying to guard her body from further harm. He threw a dirty towel at her and ordered her to clean up her "mess." He warned her that if she told anyone, he would kill her.

He got into her face with another fist ready and gritted his teeth with another threat. *"You better come up with a good story, little girl."*

Diana shut her eyes tightly as she ran her fingers through her hair. She pulled on strands until the pain awoke her. She silently screamed. A different distraction was what she needed. She turned her body to face the other side of her room.

The book just laid on the carpet, patiently waiting. She exhaled deeply. *Might as well get the next chapter done and out of the way.* She opened the book to Chapter 20: *The Wolf's Heart.*

Chapter 19

*C*hapter 20: The Wolf's Heart

It was early, not that it mattered. The sky was dark and had wept for days, leaving no shred of light. The earth became soft and soulless. Even if she had found a way to escape, it wouldn't have taken him long to catch up to her. Unlike the rest of his thralls, she was his new "favorite," and he was saving her for last.

It was a quick and painless journey. Although the words Diana read were frightening, she went in carefree. At that point, she didn't care what the book had in store for her . . . that is, until she found herself in a dark, rusty cage.

She appeared to be in a dingy longhouse that was in terrible shape. The walls were made of wood and turf. She guessed she had found herself in Viking territory, but Diana couldn't make out the nation. It was mostly quiet, but she did hear horses and a few people speaking quietly outside. She couldn't make out what they were saying, though. It was mostly dark inside, but the red flames of the hearth revealed some of her surroundings.

Two battered women were shackled to the wall across from her. One was slightly smaller than the other, and they looked to be about Diana's age. Light, feathery hair stuck out wildly from behind the leather masks strapped to their faces. They held onto each other as their naked, injured bodies shivered for warmth.

To her left, a giant man grunted in his sleep. The hideous creature—maybe an ogre of some kind?—seemed comfortable in his shit hole of a bed.

Diana wrapped her hands around the cold bars that confined her, but pain branching from her wrists to her elbows stopped her from tugging too hard. She looked down and saw she was covered in cuts and bruises. Loose, gray rags barely covered her cold, injured body.

The clanking noises the cage made as she moved startled her fellow captives. With their mouths covered, they could only motion frantically for her to quiet down. The man rolled over to his side, but luckily didn't wake up.

Her cage was the size of small box, with little room to move. She couldn't even stand. "Bookmark," Diana whispered.

Everything paused, but she still couldn't get out. When she heard The Narrator speak, he didn't sound like his usual, carefree self.

"I'm just as clueless as you are."

A shiver ran down her spine. "What do you mean?"

"Nobody has made it this far into the book . . . and neither have I. I can't tell you what's going to happen next."

"What?" Diana panicked.

"I'm really sorry," he said. "I really wish I could help you. This situation looks horrible."

"Are you joking? Please tell me this is a joke."

"I'm not joking," he said gloomily. "I'll be watching you, but I also feel constrained."

"What do you mean?" she whisper-yelled.

The chapter resumed as the bookmark ran out. The man woke up from his slumber with a daunting grin revealing his disgusting brown teeth.

"Ahh, my women are awake. Ready for another day of fun?" he teased as he played with his long ashy beard. "Well, fun for me. Certainly not for you."

He pulled the base of the smaller woman's chain, dragging her weak body toward him. His blood-soaked table held several instruments of torture. Each appeared to be handcrafted, designed specifically to inflict maximum horror and pain, and well-used. The woman screamed under the cloth that gagged her. Diana was scared beyond belief, but she had to do something to stop him.

"Leave her alone, you fucking monster!" Diana yelled as she grabbed onto her bars.

The Narrator panicked. "Diana, what the hell are you doing?"

"He must be stopped!" she yelled. "This is too much!"

The startled man dropped the chain. He allowed the girl to crawl past him, only to return her to her wall. She whimpered as the other woman held her. His face turned to Diana before he walked to his table and cleared everything off. He laughed menacingly as he unlocked her cage. Diana had nowhere to hide. She hardly had any room to move and there was only one hatch, which he blocked with his large frame.

"I guess you want to do this the hard way," her captor said with a phlegmy laugh. "Excellent."

His callused hand went in first and grabbed the back of her head. Her scalp burned. She held onto the bars as tightly as possible, but his grip was too strong. Within seconds, he ripped her out of the cage and slammed her body against the table. He didn't need rope. His heavy body was enough to pin her down. He smacked her across the face, bloodying her nose and mouth. The pain was excruciating.

"Not today, asshole!" She kneed him in the groin, but it didn't give her enough time to roll off and escape. He yanked her back into place and smacked her even harder. She couldn't breathe. Her body wanted to give out.

He laughed as he ripped off her clothes. "I'll show you a monster," he grunted.

"No!" she cried. She had to find a way to escape. "Bookmark," she wailed.

Everything paused again, but she couldn't move from the table. Her captor hovered over her with his plan set into motion. She cried out to The Narrator.

"Please, please get me out of here!"

"Diana, I can't," he whimpered. "You already used your emergency escape."

"Please," she cried. "Please find a way. I'm so scared!"

"Me, too." She could hear the pain in his voice. "But no matter what, I'll be here with you. You're gonna have to be brave!"

"No, I can't! Please don't let him do this to me!"

"Diana, I'm going to leave you for *just* a moment! I'm going to try to find an escape portal for you!"

"Don't leave me," she cried out. "Please!"

The chapter resumed again. She screamed as the man wrapped his hand around her throat. He squeezed tightly to silence her. She tried to move his hand away, but she couldn't get it to budge with the little energy she had left. He struck her once more before he laughed and untied his trousers. With the same hand, he positioned himself between her thighs. Her vision darkened with exhaustion.

A loud howling from outside temporarily ceased his vile attempt. Moments later, they heard villagers cry and scream for their lives. The ferocious packs of wolves, led by their masters, unleashed chaos in their wake. Every man, woman, and child fell victim to their vicious assault. The man quickly pulled his trousers up and rummaged through his collection of weapons. He grabbed his bearded axe and waited by the door. Diana just laid there, motionless. She tried clenching on to the last bit of her clothing, but she was too weak to even cover herself. The shackled women fell to the ground, defenseless. What hell was coming for them this time?

A beastly figure entered the doorway. His striking dark features caught Diana's eye immediately. Clad in black fur that enveloped his shins, waist, and arms, he exuded an aura of mystery and strength. His armor and cloak, as dark as night itself, added to his enigmatic allure. With his long raven hair partially tied back, he seemed almost human at first glance. However, the presence of fangs and tail unmistakably revealed his wolf-like nature. His distinctive pointy ears, reminiscent of elf ears, seemed to have caught the sound of her screams. His emerald eyes intensified as he noticed her naked, injured body.

The captor grunted as he held his axe high. He then spoke in his Norse tongue. "Úlfr, I will kill you!"

The Úlfrdraugr—wolf-men that raided their lands—were fierce warriors who battled evil mortals and other creatures to maintain the balance of nature. By the gods' decree, they were appointed as guardians of the forests. Diana shook with fear as the Úlfr drew his sword with his clawed hands. He met her gaze, then looked back at his enemy with fury.

The captor laughed malevolently. "So, you came for a treacherous whore?"

The Úlfr's sword glowed blue as it charged with power and strength. He grunted as he swung his sword and shattered the chains attached to the wall beside him. The women were freed, but still doomed like the rest. Some villagers may have been brave enough to put up a good fight, but they were severely outnumbered.

"This ends now," he growled.

The captor didn't stand a chance. His fanged opponent hoisted his sword up and through. Blood sprayed from his groin to his jugular. The last thing that his ugly face saw was his manhood and guts sprawled all over the floor. If time was not so valuable, he would have received the slower, painful death he undoubtedly deserved.

After sheathing his sword, the Úlfr rushed over to Diana.

She used her arms to shield her face and screamed the moment he tried to grab her. He yanked the cloak off his back with one arm as he kept her secured with his other. He held her up for only a moment to wrap it around her and then lifted her off the table with his strong arms.

Her screams faded into small whimpers when his hand held the side of her head against his chest. He pressed his lips against her temple. The warmth of his breath soothed her skin.

"Be still," he whispered.

Her eyes started to feel heavy as he carried her away. His thick cloak enveloped her in warmth. She could hear his comrades laugh as their wolves chased down and devoured their mortal enemies.

"Spare no one," her Úlfr savagely commanded. In his eyes, they all needed to be held accountable. They needed to feel his wrath. Every home in that village was invaded and torched to the ground. When they had their fill, they traveled north, and she drifted into a deep sleep.

They had a long journey ahead. It would take several moons to travel back to their den. The clouds darkened, and the frigid air smelled of snow. They needed to stop and rest for the evening. Drifting in and out of sleep, Diana remembered feeling thirsty at one point and mumbled something that he couldn't make out. And then she remembered his warm lips pressing gently against hers.

Another wolf-man called out to him as they approached a nearby stream. "Sko, is this where we rest?"

Sko closed his eyes and sniffed to evaluate it. "The water is clean enough. Set camp," he commanded.

They hauled their supplies and pitched tents made of canvas and animal hide. Before nightfall, they set several firepits that warmed their surroundings. The sweet smell of meat awakened her senses. Diana opened her eyes and found herself nestled in a heap of fur for comfort.

She shook as she held up her weight with one arm. When she could sit herself up, she lifted the furry pelt that covered her naked body. Her injuries had been cleaned with ointment and carefully wrapped with cloth, but she didn't remember anyone touching her.

She looked around and found herself alone. Beside her was a neatly folded set of clothes. They were simple: A white camise, a long deep blue skirt, and boots insulated with fur. Diana wanted to leave, but she could hardly move. Suddenly, she heard voices outside of her tent. She peeked through the small slit where the sheets met.

Two wolf-men stood by a fire. The one who appeared to be slightly older had short, silver hair and pale blue eyes. His companion had brownish-red hair with golden eyes. They were roasting what appeared to be a wild boar.

"He insisted that we cook this for her," the younger one grunted.

"Mortals are complicated. They cannot eat raw flesh," the other one advised. "Imagine having a fever and losing control of your bowels at the same time."

"She should have been good as dead, you know." He scoffed as he turned the rod.

"Shh!" his companion whispered. "If Sko were to hear you—"

"We serve him, not her," the younger one said, although quieter than before.

"She is his mate!" his elder retorted. "We do serve her!"

"She was the one who left him! She's unfit to be his! How could he choose a mortal, let alone a weak one? This is the third time that she has left him!"

His friend sighed. "Do you ever ask yourself why?"

The younger wolf-man growled. "Are you saying that we forced her to leave?"

"Yes, we have."

His friend spat into the flame. "I never said anything to her!"

"No, but a lot of us have. Our tribes have denounced their union, and several members have accused our leader of being a traitor. Some have plotted his death. Others have contemplated war. We are dividing. The majority have harassed her into leaving him."

His friend settled on the ground. He used a stick to poke the wood under the dancing flames. "I suppose we have then. She left to spare him—to spare us—all the trouble?"

His friend nodded. "Do you understand now?"

"I do."

"As soon as you have a mate of your own, you'll know what it's like to have that unbreakable bond." His companion gave him a smile. "Sko loves her, and he will always love her. So when I implore you to be nice to her, I mean it."

Hearing Sko's story made Diana weep. It was a forbidden love story with major consequences. Despite the fact his "mate" had left him multiple times, he still chose her over his kind, his tribe, his position as their leader. *So, he* was *looking for her. He still loves her after all of that? I don't know anything about her and yet, I can understand how she must have felt. Still, it's horrible to leave someone who loves you that much.*

The Narrator's whisper made her flinch. "Diana, don't say a word! They have excellent hearing!"

She looked up and nodded. She was ready to ask him what took him so long.

"I found you a portal. Don't you dare ask me how! You can thank me later. Just listen to me very carefully. To your left, you can crawl under the tent. Just go straight until you see a hill. Beneath it, there is a ravine. The portal will be there."

Diana wiped her tears and nodded. *I must leave. I can't stick around and cause more trouble.* She struggled as she dragged herself off the bed of fur. Putting on clothes without wincing was just as challenging. She could barely walk. *If I walk very slowly, maybe they won't notice me.*

She wrapped a pelt around her shoulders and back. *Maybe I'll be inconspicuous with these.* She poked her head out first and didn't see anyone in her path.

The sky was dark, but the moon lit up the night. The air was cold, and the ground was covered with snow. She rushed out as fast as she could. Diana could hear the other wolf-men talking at their campfires. Little did she know, they had spotted her instantly. They either didn't care that she was leaving or they were confident she wasn't going to get far. Their leader would be returning soon. Regardless, she was in fact, safe.

She came to a halt when she saw a pack of wolves pass her by, at least seven of them. Despite the initial tension, nothing happened. They glanced at her briefly, then continued on their way. It seemed that her scent had been recognized, causing no alarm or aggression from them. In her moment of stillness, she pondered if they were mere pets for the wolf-men and found herself puzzled by their decision to spare her life. *So, they're okay with me?*

The moonlight revealed the outline of the hill. From there, she could trace the guiding light. Diana knew she was heading down the right path. There was nobody in sight. The only thing she heard was the wind rattling the tall trees. She looked up and whispered to The Narrator.

"Thank you for doing this for me."

"You're welcome," he murmured. "I'm sorry that I couldn't rescue you sooner."

"I seriously can't ask you how you were able to do this?"

The Narrator gave her a long grunt. "It's complicated. I found a way out by disputing the last rule, as it was not going to be 'pleasurable' for you. I don't know what consequences we will face in the future."

Her eyes widened. "Consequences?"

"I don't know. Usually when a rule is broken or manipulated, there are repercussions. I have a bad feeling about this."

"What you said earlier," Diana gulped, "about how nobody, not even you, had made it this far into the book. Tell me how that is even possible. Is there something that I'm missing here?"

"Every host is different and has different goals. Most have finished early. You are definitely missing something, but it's up to you to figure out what."

Diana sighed. "Can you at least give me a clue?"

"Nope. You, out of all people, should know that's not how life works."

She probed further. "Is it a riddle? An object?"

"Come to think of it, I already gave you somewhat of a clue."

"What do you mean?"

"You asked me a question. I answered it. Figure it out."

She rolled her eyes. She was about to say something smart, but noticed the ravine and quickly made her way to the base. The portal revealed itself a few feet away, although it had more of a haunting appearance this time. Its circular gate, which normally glowed green, spindled with red hurtles of electricity that zapped in all directions. She could feel the static almost pulling her in. Diana felt like she was about to walk into a nightmare. She tightened her pelt to feel more secure.

"This is different," she whispered. "Why?"

"This was the best one I could find. I'm sorry. You'll still end up home. But like I said, I don't know the repercussions."

She looked down and nodded with regret. Before she could take another step, she was hindered by a loud yet familiar voice.

"No!" he howled.

She immediately spun around. Sko leapt off the hill and flew through the air. He drew his sword from its scabbard. Once again, it glowed blue, but more fiercely and fully charged. It pulsated as he raised it over his head. His back arched and his arms tightened for a wider blow. She jumped out of the way before he swung. The blue light radiated a galvanic current that slashed through and obliterated the gate! It dissipated fully before he landed on his feet.

"W-what just happened?" The Narrator stuttered. "How was he able to see it?"

He swung his sword over his head again, though only to sheath it. Sko rushed over, looking terrified. She nearly collapsed over the sharp rocks beneath her, but he managed to catch her arms. His grip was firm but gentle. She trembled in his grasp while he straightened her to her feet. He then pulled her close to his chest and wrapped his strong arms around her. She could feel his beating heart against her head as his warm body quaked. A tear dropped from his chin and landed on her cheek. Diana looked up to see his face. *Wait . . . is he crying?*

Before she knew it, he swept her off her feet and carried her away from the jagged terrain. She didn't fight him, nor did she want to. When she looked up at him again, he turned his attention elsewhere. He obviously didn't want her to see his tears. She was stunned and, at the same time, she knew she had hurt him. As soon as they made it back to his tent, he gently placed her back on the furs she awoke in. The soft glow of the campfire outside cast a warm, dim light inside the tent, illuminating everything clearly. He turned his back to her and removed his armor, fur clothing, and his scabbard. Diana heard him quietly grunting as he tossed everything aside until he was down to a simple undergarment, which only revealed his long, black tail.

He maintained his composure, and his tone remained firm. "Don't ever leave me again."

Diana gulped as she held her knees close to her chest. She tried to look away, but she couldn't help herself. Her eyes were fixed on his tall, strong physique. His bronze skin contoured the shape of his muscles. Every scar on his body had a story to tell. He tossed his long, black hair over his back while he watched her from the corner of his eye. Diana tightened her grip around her legs and pressed her chin against her knees. She felt confused. *He's beautiful . . . and dangerous. He rescued someone who broke his heart and then slaughtered an entire village. What is he planning to do with me?*

"You're safe here." His voice had softened.

Sko turned to face her. His green eyes flickered with passion as he gave her a reassuring smile. The moment she felt his gaze, she turned away. When he was about to take a step forward, another wolf-man entered their tent. Diana recognized him instantly. *It's the one who complained about me—or her, rather.* They both turned their attention to him as he held a bark plate of cooked food with one hand and a mazer of water with the other. He looked at Sko for approval.

"Will this do?" he asked.

Sko nodded and motioned for him to serve her. Diana recoiled to the other side of the pelts. She remembered what he had said earlier: "*Should have been as good as dead.*"

He placed the food beside her and forced a smile. She didn't know whether he was putting on an act for his leader or whether he was at least trying to change his mind about her.

"I hope this food is to your liking," he said with a worried tone, "and I must apologize if it's not. I've never cooked meat before."

"Thank you . . . for going out of your way," Diana responded timidly.

His ears perked up with surprise. It was the first time she had spoken to him, especially with such politeness. Her kind words made him smile naturally.

"My love, please eat," Sko instructed her. "You must regain your strength."

The boar was, in fact, delicious. Before the wolf-man was dismissed, Sko patted him on the shoulder and gave a smile of gratitude for his genuine attempt to make amends.

By the time Sko faced her, there was not even a morsal left. He couldn't help but chuckle as he made his way toward her. "It looks like he did a fine job with the boar."

She felt uneasy when he approached her from behind. Her body tensed as his hands started to undress her, causing her to instinctively pull away. Taking a gentle approach, he held her shoulders before carefully untying her camise. "You need me to look after those wounds," he explained softly.

Diana could feel her heart pounding through her ears. Her body quaked the moment he touched her bare skin. Her breaths became shallow and more frantic, gasping for air, the panic gripping her like a vise. The fear of being attacked again consumed her thoughts, leaving her feeling vulnerable and exposed. She held her arms together, covering her breasts.

His embrace enveloped her, pulling her close against his chest. The warmth of his body comforted her as she felt the steady rhythm of his heartbeat against her back. With her head nestled beneath his chin, his soft whisper reassured her, "It's okay."

He held her until their breaths were synchronized, creating a moment of calm. When she finally felt more secure, he slowly released her and brushed her long, wavy hair aside. He inspected her body. His rough hands delicately traced the sides of her arms before reaching her waist. Diana closed her eyes and quietly held a breath in.

"You're healing well, as expected. Are you in any pain?"

Diana could feel the numbing opiate he used for her cuts taking hold. She hardly felt anything besides the soreness on her face. She slowly shook her head.

"Good." Sko's lips pressed against the top of her head.

His warm breath, a tender gesture against her hair, provided solace in the midst of her grief. Yet, it couldn't erase the weight of her sorrow that lingered.

His arms wrapped around her stomach as he leaned his head down beside hers. "Are you still not talking to me?"

Her voice shook as she spoke. "Th-thank you for rescuing me."

Diana's emotions overwhelmed her as tears streamed down her face. Despite her character's actions, she was grateful that Sko had found her when he did. She covered her face with her hands, overcome with sobs, reflecting on the kindness that had come to her aid in her time of need.

He turned her around and held her close. "Shh. . . It's okay. I'm here."

"You came for me," she cried.

"Of course I did."

"Why?"

He lightly jerked his head back. "Why do you think? I love you." He pulled her hands from her face and kissed them. "You are mine. Until my last breath, you are mine."

Her teary eyes retreated to the fur they knelt on. She felt too ashamed to look at him. *He has no clue who I am. If he truly knew, he wouldn't say that.*

He slowly guided her wrists around his neck and planted soft kisses on the bruise beneath her eye. Oddly enough, they didn't hurt. In fact, his gentle affection made her feel the opposite. She closed her eyes and let out a small exhale. His lips traveled down her cheek and then to her jaw. The sound of his slow, heavy breathing followed by each kiss sent signals of pleasure below her hips. She wanted to give in to him. She wanted him to take her right then and there, but she stopped herself the moment his lips met hers.

Her lips trembled as tears flowed. "I'm sorry. You shouldn't love me. You mustn't."

"What do you mean? How could you say something like that?"

She turned away from him and remembered the last time she was this beaten down. The same old memory of her father flashed before her eyes. She could still hear his screaming rattling in her head: *"You deserve nothing!"*

Sko's hand cupped her cheek, slowly guiding her to back to him. "Hey. . . Look at me."

Her eyes remained low. "I don't deserve anything. I don't deserve you or your love."

His eyes narrowed with bewilderment. "What?"

"You shouldn't be with someone so pathetic and weak. You deserve better and—"

He pulled her against him once more. "Stop," he pleaded. "Stop."

Sko's arm wrapped around her waist as he ran his fingers through the back of her hair. She could hear his heart throbbing beneath his chest as he trembled. She lifted her head and met his captivating eyes, which ached to remedy all her sorrows.

His soft voice gave her comfort. "My love, let go of your pain. I will happily receive it."

He tightened his grip as he pulled her head toward his. The way he held her, caressed her, and kissed her liberated her spirit. She accepted his warm embrace with her own and then wept on his shoulder. The release was what she needed. When she collected herself, she grabbed him and kissed him back.

"Please," he urged, "don't ever say such things about yourself, for they are false. You are everything that I want and more."

Diana nodded as she wiped away a tear from his face. She wanted to make things right and mend his broken heart. "I'm so sorry that I hurt you. I won't ever do that again. I promise."

He cracked a smile, but pain escaped from his voice. "All that matters is that you're back and you're safe in my arms. I was worried. I was so afraid that I was going to lose you forever. You must promise me that you will never leave my side again."

His alluring, green eyes drew her closer. Their lips nearly touched. Her hands stroked his soft hair as he awaited her answer. *Could I stay?* She imagined a life with him, the possibility of endless love. She knew that after making love, the portal would reveal itself, but what if she declined to exit? And the portal—how did he see it?

"My love?" he whispered.

"Sko, that moment in the ravine—"

He pulled his head back. "You were in grave danger. I could smell it in the air."

Smell it? He is exactly like a wolf. "So you know what it was?"

He shook his head as he slightly bared his fangs. "I didn't, nor did I see its form. All I knew was that it had a mouth. By the gods, I wasn't going to let it have you."

"I see." *He was only trying to protect me.*

"This world is full of monsters…" He leaned his head against hers and sighed. "You have my solemn word that I will always protect you. I will always love you."

His words melted her. *He is different from the others.* Diana caressed his smooth face before she pressed her lips against his. She could feel the heat of his body warming hers, making her feverish. She gasped when he pulled away from her, parting lips to kiss the side of her neck. She moaned the moment she felt his brutish hands squeeze her curves. With a single pull of his hand, her long skirt dropped beneath her feet. Diana tossed it aside as her camise began to slip from her shoulders. He delicately traced the curve of her waist before swiftly removing the garment over her head.

His strong hands, conveying power and tenderness, effortlessly lifted her bottom as she instinctively wrapped her legs around his hips. He held her above him, his lips tracing a path towards her breasts. She inhaled deeply, her breath mingling with the earthy scent of his hair as she embraced his head tightly.

After what felt like just a moment, he lowered her to meet his lips before he grinded himself in between her thighs. She moaned as she felt his love extending for her. The intimate moment was filled with tension as he gently laid her down and removed his undergarment. His eyes never wavered from hers as he hovered over her.

He kissed her lips once more before he whispered in her ear. "Promise me, my love."

Diana gasped as his kisses traveled south. She closed her eyes, releasing tears of pleasure. *I love you.*

"I promise," she moaned. "I promise that I'll never leave you. I promise that I'll stay with you . . . forever."

"Diana, you can't," The Narrator said, disheartened.

They made love for the entire night. Only this time, Diana felt comfortable expressing herself fully. Sko made sure of that. His attentiveness to her needs and wants was remarkable. She pondered whether he possessed a mind-reading ability, or it was the wolf within him that allowed him to perceive beyond typical human senses.

When they were finally spent, they held each other until they drifted to sleep. He kept her safe in his arms as she nestled into his chest. Green specks of light flickered for her attention, but she pretended she didn't see. The Narrator urged her to leave, but she ignored him. She chose to stay.

It was before dawn when Sko awoke to the sound of strong winds approaching. His comrades yelled at a formidable force outside. He immediately grabbed his sword and held it steady in front of him.

The ruckus jolted Diana from her slumber. Immediately, she felt a strong yet familiar pressure hit her abdomen. It was the same pressure she felt when the book first sucked her in.

"No!" she winced.

"What's happening?" he yelled.

She held onto him for dear life; she knew what was coming. The winds tore their tent to shreds, leaving nothing but remnants of material that rapidly spun around them. Sko's sword was instantly pulled from his hands. They were surrounded. Diana's scream echoed through the wind as she was lifted off the ground. Sko rushed to her aid, grasping her tightly, but the force was overwhelming. He whimpered as he felt her slowly being ripped from his grasp. Tears streamed down her face as she held onto him tightly for one final moment.

"I love you," he said as he wept.

As she slipped out of his reach, she heard him wail out one final word that broke her heart. "Diana!"

She found herself back where she started. On her bed, in her room, and all alone. She rushed through the book to find the same chapter, but just like the others, it was erased.

"No! This can't be happening!" she cried. "He called out my name! He knew who I was! This can't be happening! No!"

Her body collapsed over the book. She begged to see him once more, but no matter how hard she cried, it wouldn't make an exception for her.

"Sko! Give him back to me!" She shook the book. "Give him back, damn it!"

Chapter 20

Γ he alarm went off at seven, but Diana was already awake. As much as she needed to rest, she couldn't. She couldn't get over the last chapter. She couldn't get over Sko. She replayed everything that happened over and over, but she still couldn't connect the dots. *He knew me, but how?*

What the book did to her was brutal. She went through most of the stages of grief in record time. "This had to be some sort of sick joke," she decided as she cried into her pillow. "That damn book is getting back at me for the grill."

Bitterness and frustration soon took sorrow's place. "I can't fucking believe this! This is bullshit!" She slammed the book on the floor, not caring whether it would come back to life to haunt her.

It didn't react, which pissed her off even more. "You fuck!"

The love that she felt from Sko was unmatched. She began pacing around the room. "He wasn't like the others. If only I hadn't used my stupid wish right away!" She pressed her hands against her head and grunted. "I didn't even get the chance to say goodbye to him. I didn't get the chance to tell him . . ."

Diana leered at the book again, and then she remembered the old gypsy-witch who had cursed her. "If only I knew where you were hiding, I would share more than just words with you."

She flinched when she heard a loud knock at her door. Jordan's cheery voice followed. "Hey girl, may I come in?"

Diana wiped her face and quickly hid the book under her pillow. She forced a grin to conceal her sadness. "Sure!"

Jordan walked in with a few garment bags. "I found some outfits that you may want to try on!"

Diana plastered on a wider smile. *That's right! Today is important. I need to stay focused on that.* "Thank you, Jordan. You shouldn't have."

Jordan stared at her face. "Everything okay?"

When Diana returned to their world, her cuts and bruises disappeared along with the chapter. All that remained were her puffy eyes. It was evident that she had been up all night. "I just couldn't sleep, so I ended up . . . reading."

"I'll bring you my ice pack," Jordan said. "I also have this really good moisturizer that you can use for your face. I'll leave it on my vanity with that eyeshadow you like."

"Thank you."

Jordan smiled as her hand reached for the door. "I'll whip up some blueberry pancakes for you. Can't go to work on your first day with an empty stomach!"

Before she left, Diana grabbed her arm and pulled her in for a tight embrace. Jordan was a bit puzzled, but reciprocated. Diana realized that if the book had granted her wish to remain in the last chapter, she never would have seen her best friend again. Losing her would have been devastating. *It would have been a shitty price to pay. I'll never take our friendship for granted again.*

"What's this all about?"

"You're seriously the greatest friend."

Jordan chuckled and rolled her eyes. "I know."

"And you were right about everything," Diana murmured.

Jordan raised her brows. "Oh?"

"Everything," she repeated.

"Can you be a little more specific?"

Diana shook her head. "If it's okay with you, I would like to move out in a month—after I get the hang of this job, that is."

"You know you can stay here as long as you want."

"Thank you. I might need your help with finding an apartment, too."

"So, you'll be living alone then?"

Diana sighed. "You want me to say it, don't you?"

"Of course I do!" Jordan laughed. "This is the moment that we've been waiting for! I want you to say it loud and proud!"

"Okay," Diana took a deep breath and fanned her face with her hands. "Okay, here it goes...Tom and I are *over*!"

It was a glorious morning full of laughter and pancakes. Before Diana left for orientation, she studied herself in Jordan's full-length mirror. Jordan helped her pick the right outfit—a fitted, deep violet dress that ended at her knees. She wore a black blazer over it with matching shoes. Her dark wavy hair was carried over to one shoulder as she applied more blush. Focusing was difficult. Every time the soft hairs brushed against her cheeks, she imagined Sko kissing them instead. She tightly gripped onto the handle and let out a long breath.

The chances of seeing him again were unlikely. She yearned for him, but she knew she had to move on. She had her own life. She was finally loved the way she had always wanted to be loved. *How many people can say they've experienced that?*

She knew that she had to be strong, so she made promises to herself—and to him. *I promise that I will carry your heart with me wherever I go. I promise that I will never say hurtful words to myself ever again. I promise that no matter what happens in my life, I will know that I am worthy, capable, and beautiful.* She smiled at herself for finally accepting such a high standard for her own happiness. *This is what self-love must feel like.*

Orientation was just as she imagined—exciting. On a personal level, she got to know Jerry a little better. After lunch, he escorted Diana to her office and introduced her to her personal staff and assistants. It all seemed surreal; she had never had people working for her before. She felt like she was in the end of *Working Girl* and wanted to call Jordan from her large office. The entire day was surprisingly amazing. She learned the ins and outs of her position. Everyone on her floor was so friendly, and, other than Jerry, she was basically her own boss.

She was there for a full day and didn't realize where the time had gone. After she signed off, she left the parking lot feeling more assured that things were going to be just fine and that everything that happened had been a blessing in disguise. For that entire day, she did not receive any calls or texts from Tom, nor did she care. She laughed at the thought of him trying to "punish" her with the silent treatment.

When she made it back home, Jordan and Leif had prepared a celebratory dinner in her honor. They dined in the kitchen and discussed what would happen next.

"So, you're still going to see Tom tomorrow?" Leif's eyes widened with curiosity.

"Yeah," Diana sighed as she rolled her eyes. "I need to tell him—straight to his face—that I don't want to be with him and that I won't marry him."

Jordan nearly choked on her steak. "Hold up! What?"

Leif's jaw dropped.

"Oh yeah," Diana nervously giggled. "I didn't want to tell anyone that he proposed. I didn't give him an answer, and he's still pretty upset about it."

Jordan wiped the corner of her mouth with her napkin. Diana chuckled at her friend's odd expression. "Why are you staring at me like that?"

"Umm, did he even give you a ring?"

"Yeah, but it seriously didn't feel right . . . and it has a ruby in it."

Jordan squinted her eyes as her lips curled with disgust. "You hate red! It makes me wonder—"

Leif shook his head. "Jordan, don't say it."

Diana gasped. "Oh! Ha! You think it was for Gwen?"

Jordan confidently poured herself another glass of merlot. "Think about it for a second. They were madly in love with each other until the 'incident,' and then right after, he had a ring for you? Something isn't adding up. Also, red is the signature color of—"

"Of whores!" Diana shouted.

Jordan and Leif laughed aloud as she continued.

"How befitting for her! Oh my God!"

Leif smirked. "And he's mad at you for not giving him an answer? I would like to meet this guy."

Jordan turned to her. "Do you need us to be there for support? We can come with if you need backup."

Diana shook her head. "I don't think so. Knowing how he is, he'll probably make it easier for me to leave. At that point, it won't be my problem anymore."

"I really do like seeing this side of you." A giggle escaped from Jordan's lips. "You've never told me what had this effect on you."

Diana took a sip of her wine as she thought of what to say. She had to come up with something other than the book. "I think it was a combination of everything. It was like I was forced to start over and grow up, you know?"

Leif clinked his glass with hers and lifted it over his head. "That makes sense. A swift reboot is what we need sometimes."

After dinner, Jordan and Leif went out to the movies. Diana wasn't in the mood, so she stayed in. She tossed and turned in bed, consumed by thoughts of Sko's fate after the last chapter. Was he going to be alright, or had he been erased along with the chapter? The uncertainty lingered, keeping her awake with worry.

At the same time, she had a lot to think about. *What do I need to do to be officially done with this book? I'm ready for everything to be over!*

She rolled her eyes and yelled aloud. "Fine! Let's play another game of Fuck Around and Find Out, shall we?" She opened the book to the next chapter. The title automatically annoyed her.

Chapter 21: The Damsel

He was still aggrieved and demanded retribution for her actions. Finding her was not an easy task. He crossed the sea that divided their lands. He ordered a handful of his best warriors to travel by his side. Nothing was going to stop him from capturing her . . .

Diana instantly found herself hiding behind large boulders in the middle of some rocky terrain. Seven men rode on their horses. Six of them wore black tunics and black veils that covered their faces. The seventh man, who also had a covered face, wore white and gold.

"Keep searching. Don't stop until you have something to report," he commanded his men.

Diana's clothing hinted at the ancient era setting of the chapter. The Grecian sandals she wore were flimsy and torn, mirroring the state of her pale-yellow garments that engulfed her. Her loose attire was secured by a thin rope that acted as a belt, emphasizing her slender waist. *So, I'm easy to spot and I can't run anywhere. Nice.*

"I'm glad you're back," The Narrator said, sounding tentative.

"Bookmark!" Diana sighed. "I'm not."

"I know," he murmured. "Diana, it was beyond my control. You knew that you had to leave."

"He knew my name," she barked. "I know that you know something, so fess up!"

The Narrator hesitated. "He . . . he wasn't supposed to. I don't know how he broke out of character and called you by your name, but he's gone. Completely vanished."

Her eyes widened. *I was expecting a real explanation, at the very least.*

"Vanished?" she yelled. "Like he no longer exists?"

"I don't know," he lamented. "This has never happened before. After you were forced to leave, I tried to locate him in the book, but his chapter was permanently erased. It's as if he never existed."

She held a clenched fist over her heart. Her eyes teared up as The Narrator continued.

"Sko and his chapter were new. I highly doubt that you and his mate had the same name by coincidence. He was different, wasn't he? You felt a deeper connection with him."

Diana nodded. "It's hard to explain. I felt completely transparent with him. He read me like an open book. And for the first time, I didn't feel uncomfortable or ashamed. He accepted my feelings. He accepted me for me."

"I'm truly sorry. I wish I could give you real answers. I wish I could tell you what's going to happen here, but of course, this one is also new to me. Watch out! It's starting again in three, two, one."

The chapter resumed. At that point, Diana didn't care whether she was discovered. She was fed up. She stood atop the rocks and waved her arms like a dealership air dancer. Her movements were wild and free, matching the untamed spirit of the wind and the rugged scenery around her. *It's not like I can escape either way.* She was certain she was meant to be found.

The Narrator yelled at her. "Diana, what the hell are you doing?"

She rolled her eyes to the sky. "You don't even know what's going to happen."

She called out to the men. "Hey! I'm here! Come and get me!"

"Diana!" The Narrator panicked.

The man in white raised his sword in the air. "Hold her there! I will kill her myself!" The horses galloped their way toward her at full speed.

Despite her fear, Diana stood her ground. She felt a knot in her stomach and her heart raced, but she steeled herself, closing her eyes tightly. In mere seconds, a sharp sound sliced through the wind, followed by a piercing cry.

The sudden and violent image that greeted her as she opened her eyes was one that she would never forget. The man closest to her had fallen off his horse, a spear lodged in his back. His final breath escaped with a giant grunt as his body thudded against the unforgiving ground. Diana's mouth hung open as her hands dropped to her sides. The other riders reacted quickly, pulling on their reins to bring their horses to an abrupt stop. The sound of their horses neighing filled the air, signaling their sudden halt.

Diana looked around, but she couldn't see anyone else.

"Who did that?" their leader shouted.

The sudden appearance of ten powerful hoplites clad in bronze armor and Corinthian helmets marked a pivotal moment. Their commander, distinguished by a red crest on his armor, rallied them with a fierce cry to attack.

They swiftly descended the steep hills, seamlessly dismounted on the gravel, and launched a fierce assault on their foes. This sudden and bold attack caught their enemies off guard, allowing the hoplites to strike with full force.

Diana took cover behind the boulders again. As she heard swords clashing and men screaming, she called out to The Narrator. "Am I, like, in ancient Greece or something?"

The Narrator laughed. "It seems like it." He was about to say something clever, but then noticed Diana had a visitor hovering over her. "Hey! Behind you."

When she turned to peek over the rocks, she gasped at the large, callused feet in front of her. The Greek leader stood over her and smirked. His voice was low. "So you're the one they've been searching for?"

She backed away as he jumped off a boulder and landed inches away from her. Before she could say anything, he took her arm and pulled her closer. His grasp was gentle but inescapable. It grew quiet around them. The hoplites were unmatched.

He laughed as he took off his helmet and revealed his gorgeous, chiseled face. His dark wavy hair flowed down to his neck and was braided back. His eyes, resembling the color of toasted almonds, held a certain warmth and depth. Unlike Leonidas, his face was smooth and devoid of a beard. Despite his youthful appearance, he seemed to be no younger than her, exuding a sense of maturity beyond his years. As they neared their surrendering enemies, he instinctively drew her closer to his side, their eyes fixed on four remaining foes.

"You need not to worry," he told her. "My name is Aegeus, and you're in my territory now."

The horses were separated from their masters. The men in black veils faced imminent danger as spears and swords closed in on them. Their leader, dressed in white, scolded them for their cowardice, urging them to stand their ground. The hoplites, with discipline, awaited for their commander's signal.

"Reveal yourselves," Aegeus demanded.

Their captives unveiled their bearded faces and revealed their identities, despite their leader's initial refusal. The threat of spears near his neck compelled him to comply. Diana shook with fear after she realized who he was, then hid behind her captor.

"Bookmark," she called out. "And you better have a good explanation for this one!"

The Narrator was just as shocked as she was, but he also found it insanely humorous. He couldn't hold back his laughter. "You need to calm down!"

"I will not *calm down*! What the hell is Jafeer doing here?"

His chortling continued. "I'm not sure. Perhaps it's the fact that you didn't finish his chapter."

"What?!" she screamed. "I used that emergency escape fair and square!"

"But you also hit his head with a vase. That was not supposed to happen. He probably wants vengeance."

"No way!" she yelled. "That freak seriously went out of his way to find me and somehow made it to a different chapter? Hell no!"

There was a long pause from The Narrator.

Diana grunted in frustration. "Umm! Hello? Are you there?"

"Whoops! I forgot that you can't see me. I was shrugging my shoulders. . . You know, Persia is not that far from Greece. It's not impossible."

Diana rolled her eyes and crossed her arms in front of her. "This is unfair."

"Jafeer is losing. You'll be fine."

She deeply exhaled before the chapter resumed again. She peeked over Aegeus's shoulder. Jafeer's eyes deepened with resentment. It was clear he was still furious. He gave her a devious, threatening smirk.

Diana's arms remained crossed as she stared him down. *What a self-entitled, spoiled rotten twerp! He's not gonna get what he wants! I'm not gonna apologize, either!*

"I will take what is mine!" Jafeer barked.

"Oh yeah?" Diana screamed even louder. "And what might that be?"

"Your life!" he retorted.

Aegeus used the back of his arm to shield her. He gave Jafeer a playful glance. "Now, now, what could this celestial beauty have done to the mighty prince?"

Diana didn't hold back. She softly whispered the embarrassing details into his ear. Aegeus cackled aloud for everyone to hear. "Oh, so you ordered this damsel to take *special* care of your ass?"

Jafeer's face turned red when everyone—including his own men—laughed at him. His face got even redder after a large Greek soldier approached him with a seductive smile. "I did *not!*" Jafeer yelled. "That concubine is lying!"

"We'll see about that." Aegeus smirked and then turned to his men. "Take these captives to the city. The king will decide what to do with them."

He wrapped his arm around Diana's shoulders as he continued. "No need to wait. We'll catch up with you before nightfall."

His men grinned as if they knew what he had planned with her. They tied up their enemies and headed west. Jafeer wouldn't stop his threats, so they gagged him with his veil. Diana felt the blood rush to her cheeks when Aegeus lifted her to his horse and positioned himself behind her. He had control of the reins, and they rode to a secluded spot. It was clear that a private moment with her was all he ached for. When they arrived, he helped her off and tied the horse to a tree.

"Do you see that cave across from the waterfall?" he motioned. "Wait for me there."

Diana responded with a simple nod, nothing more. She felt his gaze follow her as she walked past him.

The cave wasn't dark; the sunlight illuminated its glistening rocky features. The air wasn't as damp as she thought it would be, and there were clear signs of habitation. She noticed a fire pit, a cot made from straw, and a few empty bowls. *This must be his secret hide-out.* His low voice slightly startled her, but not enough to make it obvious.

"We often retire here when patrols are needed. Rest assured, you are safe."

She turned to face him and noticed that his armor was already off. He was down to a simple red tunic that revealed his strong physique. Diana blushed. "Thank you for rescuing me."

Aegeus smiled. "I must say, you put up a brave front when you revealed yourself to the Persians, especially when you challenged the arrogant prince. For a woman in distress, you were very courageous."

Diana enjoyed his compliment. "Thank you."

"What's your name?"

Diana hesitated, as she didn't know how to respond. *Is it Ariana from Chapter 2 or my real name? Something else?* "My name . . . does it matter?"

Aegeus twirled a strand of her hair from her shoulder. "Are you to tell me your name, or must I earn it?"

Her voice shook. "Diana. My name is Diana."

Aegeus leaned his head forward for a kiss. "Well, Diana, a brave and fiery woman is what I've been longing for." Their lips nearly met as he took her hand and began sliding it below his stomach. "Eros has struck me . . . hard."

Diana gasped and pulled herself away. She shielded her mouth with the back of her hand and took a couple steps back.

Aegeus was stunned. Never had a woman refused his charms. His puzzled eyes stared into hers. When he took another step forward, she reversed again. Her breath quickened.

"You have no reason to fear me." He smiled. "I will not have you unless you change your mind."

Diana moved her hand away from her mouth. She was surprised he accepted rejection so easily. Although he was direct, he spoke with honesty. With a simple smile, Diana realized he would not try to persuade her.

Although there was no doubt that he would give her great pleasure, she knew she wasn't ready to start again. The last chapter and how Sko made her feel were all she could think about. Aegeus took notice of her softened expression as she stared away from him. He then grinned as if he discovered what ailed her.

"It isn't the angry prince who has your heart, is it?"

Diana was caught off guard by his question. She couldn't help but laugh and shake her head with disgust. "No, definitely not!"

"I'm relieved." He chuckled.

The Narrator cut in. "I really do like this guy. It's a shame you won't give him a go."

Her laughter and smile faded. "What's going to happen next?"

"Well, since you have made up your mind about me, I must remain honorable and take my leave." He held her hand and spoke again. "You're a free woman."

In return, she smiled and kissed his hand. "Farewell, Aegeus."

And just like that, he took his leave. Diana stood alone. The fear of being trapped in this chapter slowly crept in. The uncertainty of what lay ahead loomed over her, making her almost regret her decision.

The Narrator spoke again. "Have you figured it out?"

Diana nodded and closed her eyes. "I missed what I never had in the first place."

Vivid flashbacks of her old self manifested. She saw who she once was: A frightened, diffident, and hopeless girl. Memories of her book adventures followed.

"I thought it only existed in books and in fairytales. And I didn't want to believe in its existence because I thought I didn't deserve it."

Then, her memories of Sko came to flooding in. She remembered his strong embrace, his kiss, his soft voice whispering to her ear, the moment he said he loved her, and the moment he called out her name. She could almost feel his presence. She felt a warm glow kiss her cheeks.

"Until I met *him*," Diana said. "True love—that's what I've been missing."

"True love, hmm?" The Narrator didn't sound pleased.

Diana suddenly felt worried. *Oh shit. Did I give him the wrong answer?*

"You know . . . Damn it. I'm gonna miss you." He said with a laugh.

She sighed with relief. "I never thought I would say this, but I'm gonna miss you, too."

"Ha! I knew you were going to like me in the end. You hosts are all the same to me."

Diana crossed her arms and looked up with attitude. "Wow!"

"But I am very proud of you."

Diana smiled. "So, this is it then? This is the end?"

"Nah. It's your beginning."

"What?"

Within a blink of an eye, Diana tumbled onto her bed and sprung back up. She found herself back in her familiar world, her own room. Surprisingly, only an hour had passed since she left.

On the foot of the bed, the book glowed and began to disintegrate, emitting neon specks of light reminiscent of sparklers from her childhood. Their burning light slowly fading as they floated to the ceiling created an eerie yet mesmerizing scene. Within mere seconds, the book vanished completely, leaving behind a sense of wonder and curiosity in the air. For a brief moment, she just stood there and watched where it had been.

"It's over." Only the outline of its rectangular shape lingered on her comforter. She could hear the *Hallelujah Chorus* in her head. "I'm done!" She screamed for joy and waived her hands in the air.

Later that evening, after much dancing and singing, Diana pulled out her laptop and started typing a new story. A story about a girl—a hopeless romantic who eventually found the rarest and the most deserving love at the end. She smiled as she sipped her tea.

In the midst of it, she couldn't help but think about The Narrator's final words: "*It's your beginning.*" She wasn't sure what he meant, but she believed it was the green light to officially start over with her life.

She thought about the next morning and how she would be completely liberated from Tom. *I can't believe that I'm actually excited about this.*

Diana laughed as she typed away. *I'll just change the villain's last name.*

Chapter 21

The ice from the recent snowstorm was finally melting. It was thirty-three degrees outside, but at least the sun was shining. Diana had finally received a text from Tom, but it was only to confirm the time they were supposed to meet. She checked and rechecked her purse to ensure she had everything that she needed, especially the engagement ring.

Jordan and Leif sat on the couch in their PJs, watching his favorite movie, *Mike and Dave Need Wedding Dates*. Bandit laid comfortably beneath their feet.

Leif chuckled. "This movie cracks me up every time."

Jordan nearly choked on her coffee as she stared at the screen. "Don't tell me she's gonna do what I think she is!"

Diana laughed as she grabbed her keys. She was ready to face Tom for the final time. "Well, I'm off."

Jordan looked over and smiled. "Hey pretty lady, I see you."

Diana twirled and giggled. "I found this overcoat in your closet. I hope you don't mind."

"Of course I don't! You look amazing!"

"Well, thanks."

Leif had turned serious. "Hey, if anything happens, I want you to call us immediately."

"Yeah, we'll be ready to kick some ass," Jordan added.

"I know. Thank you."

Jordan ran from the couch to give her best friend a hug. "Raise hell for me."

The roads were still coated with black ice. It was a busy morning, as it was the weekend after Christmas, and traffic was slow. Most stores on the strip were pushing post-holiday sales. She managed to find the last parking space, farthest from the café, but that was fine. She glanced at her phone screen, which confirmed it was only five minutes past. As she made her way to the café door, she noticed Tom's Honda parked across from the café. Diana scoffed before she walked in. *His undying punctuality will no longer be a concern of mine. Life happens!*

The sweet aroma of pastries and coffee put a smile on her face. The café was busy, and the tables were full. Diana found Tom sitting at the furthest one, facing the windows. He was dressed well, sporting khakis and a navy sweater that only revealed the top of his white undershirt. He had combed his blond hair back. The last time he did that for her was on their first date. *Looks like he wants to make me swoon.* Two cups sat in front of him.

"Is this seat taken?" She smiled.

Tom looked up and almost didn't recognize her. Diana was dressed in a short denim skirt with sheer leggings and brown boots. Underneath her brown overcoat, she wore a fitted white sweater. She had left her long, perfectly wavy hair down. Her makeup was flawless. Tom fixed his gaping mouth and rose from his seat to hug her.

"Wow! You look gorgeous."

"Thanks."

He leaned in for a kiss, but she turned her head just in time. An air kiss was all he got. Diana took her seat. She could see in his eyes that Tom was taken aback by her lack of affection, but he chose not to react. He sat too and then slid her drink across the table.

"I got us our usual orders."

"That was nice of you." She took a sip. "Mmm, Christmas in a cup."

He paused, as if he was waiting for a more obvious show of gratitude. "Yeah, that was."

Diana wrapped her hands around her cup and enjoyed its warmth. "It's chilly out."

"Well, it's December so . . ."

Her eyes stared directly into his. "So, ready to talk about this?"

"Of course I am. You start."

So be it then. "Well, for the past couple of days, I have done a lot of soul-searching. I really needed time to think things through . . . for my sake. Tom, I'm really not comfortable starting over with you, so I won't."

"What?"

He looked shocked, but she maintained her confident expression. She took the engagement ring out of her purse and handed it to him. Diana knew arguing about who it was really meant for would have been a complete waste of her time. It wasn't going to change her decision. He looked down with utter disappointment as he clenched onto it tightly.

"You need more time," he said matter-of-factly. "That's okay."

"No, Tom. I don't need or want any more time. I want us to move on. We can still be friends."

"How can you do this to us?" he whispered angrily. "You would throw away an eight-year relationship?"

She took another sip. "But it was fine when you did it, right?"

He softened his tone and grabbed her hand. "I've changed. We've changed. I'm fully committed to you. I won't ever cheat on you again. I won't hurt you ever again. I thought we had already forgiven each other."

"I *have* forgiven you. I just realized that I don't want to be with you anymore."

"If you truly forgave me, then why? Cut the bullshit and answer honestly."

"I know that I deserve better."

Tom laughed as she pulled her hand away from his. "After everything that I have done for you? How about the times that I rescued you from your parents every week? Or how about when I used my life savings to move you out here with me?"

Diana rested her chin on her hands. "I appreciate all that you have done for me—"

"Bullshit!"

She continued bravely. "And now, it's time for us to move on. It's over."

"You seriously think that you deserve better?" he sneered.

Before she could answer, she heard the café's radio play a familiar artist—Haddaway. The last time she heard that song was when she fled from A BookStore, when she thought she was being cursed. This time was different. She didn't feel scared or even alone for that matter. Diana couldn't help but smile. Everything that she went through changed her for the better. *That crazy old witch was on my side all along.*

"What are you smiling about?" Tom demanded.

She got up from her seat and grabbed her purse. "Nothing. Good-bye, Tom."

As she turned away, he grabbed her wrist and yanked her closer to him. She winced in pain as he got in her face. Every customer was watching.

"You will *not* walk out on me!" he growled.

Suddenly, and without warning, Tom was shoved over the table with his arm pinned against his back. He wailed in agony.

Diana was freed! She looked up to see who was helping her—and then panicked. *No, no, no. How is this possible? It can't be Jafeer again!*

The familiar-looking man tightened his hammerlock on Tom. "So, you like putting your hands on women?" he grunted.

Diana shook as she backed away from their table. Then she felt large hands grab her shoulders from behind. She jumped from her spot as she heard another familiar voice.

"Jamal, hold him there," the new voice said. "Terry is calling the police right now."

"What?!" Tom yelled. "Diana, tell them we're fine! We were just talking!"

Diana almost fainted when she saw Terry. Only, it wasn't Terry; it was Prince Tion. She closed her eyes. *They can't be here. They weren't real!*

The man who held Diana by her shoulders gently turned her around to face him. "Lady, are you okay?"

She opened her eyes. *Holy shit. This is happening.* It was Aegeus. She couldn't make out a single word after that.

"Andrew, how is she doing?" Jamal asked.

Diana snapped back into reality the moment she heard Tom screaming again.

"Let me go! Diana, make him stop!"

When her senses returned, she turned to Jamal and spoke to him softly. "Please let him go."

Jamal gave her a serious look and then stared down Tom. "Are you sure? It sounds like he hasn't learned his lesson."

Diana held her hands together and pleaded. "Yes. He's not worth it. Please let him go."

He slightly loosened his grip. "Apologize to the lady first."

Tom cried as he was being forced to look at her. "I'm . . . sorry."

Jamal finally let Tom go, causing him to crumple to the floor. He held his arm close to his chest as sweat and tears dripped from his face. When he regained some strength, he picked himself up and walked away from the table. He couldn't look back.

Andrew then spoke loud enough for him to hear. "Don't you ever come near her again."

Tom's voice rattled with fear. "I won't."

As soon as the door closed on him, the customers clapped and cheered. Terry disconnected his call when Tom was officially out of sight. To celebrate, the café manager gave out a free round of cookies.

The three men sat with Diana until she calmed down. She was dumbfounded. They appeared to be exactly like the characters from the book, but they had their own real lives. It was weird enough to see them in regular clothing and with different haircuts, but to be talking to them all at once? Terry was a married man with a daughter on the way. Andrew had a girlfriend overseas. And Jamal . . . well, let's just say that he preferred the single life. The men had made plans to get coffee and then watch the Manchester United game at their favorite hooligan bar.

Andrew laughed as he shook his head. "I can't believe we rescued a Gunners fan."

"I think this will be our year!"

Jamal clinked his cup against hers. "You're right! Your year to be ranked fifth again."

She mocked a gasp.

Terry smiled as he pulled out his phone. "What's your number? We'll all meet for next week's game. Just don't wear your jersey! We can't guarantee your safety there."

Andrew laughed again. "Yeah, we'll definitely be outnumbered."

"Sure!" she smiled and filled them in.

That day, Diana made three amazing friends. She wasn't sure how or why it happened, but she was glad they reappeared in her life, in her world. She walked outside and wondered whether she would run into other characters. She smiled as she thought about seeing—

"Ahh!" She slipped on one of the remaining patches of ice. As gravity pulled her down, her cookie bag flew into the air. Before she crash-landed, someone broke her fall. A strong hand supported her back as the other gripped the side of her thigh. It was almost like what you would see on a *Gone with the Wind* poster. They gazed at each other for a while before he helped her to her feet.

Diana could feel her heart pounding out of her chest. *Oh my God!*

His hair was as black as she remembered, but shorter and with an undercut. He wore black utility pants and a black jacket that secured a gray knit scarf around his neck. His emerald eyes captivated her all over again. His face remained the same, only he was fully human.

"Are you all right, miss?"

His voice made her quiver. She was speechless for a moment. "Thank you."

He smiled as he picked her bag up off the sidewalk and placed it in her hands. "I think this belongs to you."

"Oh, thank you."

"Hey . . . I know you."

What? How! She bit her bottom lip. "Umm—"

"It was a few weeks ago when we had that downpour. You were crying in your car. I didn't mean to frighten you."

Diana's heart sank. She remembered vividly what happened that day and how humiliated she was after Tom broke up with her. It rained hard that morning. She took Bandit, ran to her car, and then cried hysterically over her steering wheel. A stranger had knocked on her door and had asked her if she was all right, but she freaked out and drove away.

It was him. It was Sko.

She gasped with embarrassment.

He smirked. "You know, I didn't think it was possible to be even more drenched than I was. That is, until you splashed me during your getaway. Good deeds never go unpunished, I guess."

Diana placed her hands over her cheeks. "Oh no! I am so sorry. Please let me make it up to you."

He laughed as he extended his hand. "I'm Skylor."

She blushed as she extended hers. "Diana."

Although his touch nearly melted her, she was still in shock. Her thoughts bounced all over the place. *So he already existed? Is that why he was permanently erased? This doesn't explain how everybody else got out. I hope this isn't a test. I can't do any more tests! None of this crap makes any sense.*

The only reasonable explanation that she came up with was that all the lovers from the book must have existed as potential opportunities and possible relationships had she not wasted years with Tom.

"You can make it up to me over dinner," he offered with a sexy smile. "That is, if you're not already taken."

She smiled back. "Dinner sounds lovely."

And it was. He took her out to the best tapas bistro in the city, where they talked for hours. They learned a lot about each other that evening. Apparently, Skylor worked near her apartment as an actuary. From his office, he saw a girl running in the rain with a puppy. He thought that she needed help.

It warmed her heart knowing that his first instinct was to rescue her. She felt bad for ruining his suit, but of course, he couldn't blame her. He explained how amazed he was by her courage to get out of that horrible relationship. It was a night of bliss, romance, and laughter. They didn't want it to end.

He wrapped her in his coat and put his arm around her as they kept talking on the way to their vehicles.

"So you broke her nose?"

"It was the ball, technically."

"Hahaha!"

Speaking of the homewrecker, Gwyneth not only left Tom clueless of her whereabouts, but nobody had seen or talked to her since the baseball incident.

In fact, in the middle of that Christmas snowstorm, she took shelter in an old bookstore. Its elderly owner presented her with a book to keep her mind from her troubles.

"I hate romance novels," she snarled as she grabbed the bridge of her nose. "They remind me of someone stupid I know! Do you have any horror? I would rather read something that will disgust me and give me terrorizing nightmares."

"Oh, I have something special for you, my dear. This is a lot scarier."

"This better be good, lady. I don't want to waste my money on stupid shit."

"It's a gift, my dear. I promise that you will never return . . . it."

Epilogue

A *lmost a year later*

Diana handed Jordan her bouquet behind the chapel doors. She whispered as Jordan attempted to adjust her bridesmaid dress.

"It's okay! Just hold the flowers there and nobody will notice."

"Oh, they'll notice all right." Jordan murmured. "We wanted to keep it a secret for another couple of weeks. Everyone is going to look at my belly, not at the bride."

Diana giggled. "Seriously, you're carrying it so well. I wouldn't worry about it."

Jordan then gave her a smirk as if she knew something Diana didn't. "You better get to your seat. Your man is waiting for you."

"What's that look for?"

Jordan rolled her eyes and smirked again. "Nothing."

It wasn't long before the processional began. A small ensemble of musicians played their string instruments as the doors slowly opened. The guests rose from their seats to witness the bride's grand entrance. Candlelit lanterns were placed at the side of every other pew. The flower arrangements of soft gardenias and hydrangeas enchanted the ceremony.

Jordan was the first to lead the bridesmaids. Her lavender gown flowed softly through the rose pedals beneath her feet. Leif gazed at his beautiful wife from the front pew. It had only been a few months since they eloped, and now they had a baby on the way.

From the altar, a tall, handsome, older gentleman stood with happy tears. He was finally marrying the woman of his dreams. When she approached the altar, he lifted her veil and kissed her beautiful face. The minister began his speech.

"Dearly beloved, we are gathered here today in the presence of family and friends, to join Jerry Wilcox and Sherry Whitfield in holy matrimony commended to be honorable among all..."

Diana couldn't help but smile at their joy. It was almost overwhelming. Who would have thought that an old love story between two people could come back to life against the odds? All it took was a little persuasion. It gave her hope that anything was possible.

Skylor sat beside her with his arm wrapped around her waist. He kissed her gently on the cheek as the bride and groom exchanged their vows. In his jacket, he held onto a tiny box that contained something special, something that would forever symbolize his adoration for her. And it was *not* red.

Coming Soon

The Wolf's Heart

About the Author

I'm a wife and a stay-at-home mother who lives in the countryside of the Midwest. I also have fourteen chickens which adds a touch of charm to my rural lifestyle. For the most part, I enjoy the peace and quiet of it all. I'm an artist. I enjoy drawing, painting, and writing. I'm also a former bodybuilder and I have a Bachelor's Degree in Health Education—Not that I use it. While health and fitness are still important to me, writing has always held a special place in my heart. It's a strong passion of mine. I firmly believe that you should write what you enjoy reading, and romance has always been my favorite genre.

I wrote this novel while I was going through several tough moments in my life, and I never thought I was going to have the courage to publish it. Art has always been a constant source of solace and inspiration for me. In my times of struggle, it has been a lifeline, offering a safe space for expression and reflection, ultimately playing a vital role in shaping my identity and allowing me to navigate personal challenges with resilience and creativity. As silly and absurd my novel may be, it carries fragments of my own experiences. My hope is that amidst the outlandish plot twists and quirky characters, there lies a relatable essence that can resonate with my readers on a personal level. If my novel can bring a smile to someone's face or provide a moment of escape, then I would consider it a success.